A Harvest Moon's Hope

A Pinewood Corners Sweet Romance

CAROL BABINEAUX

A HARVEST MOON'S HOPE
A Pinewood Corners Sweet Romance

Book Design by Transcendent Publishing | transcendentpublishing.com
Editing by Lori Lynn Enterprises

ISBN: 979-8-9915257-1-8

Printed in the United States of America.

Dedication

To my family and friends with love.
Thank you all for your support and for
being so understanding
when I had to cancel plans to write.

Table of Contents

Chapter 1

"*Daddy?*" *The sound of my voice echoed all around me.*

The hallway seemed to stretch out forever, like a circus funhouse, the walls closing in as the narrow floor extended endlessly forward. I forced myself to continue putting one small foot in front of the other.

Every sound seemed amplified. My stiff, white church shoes clacked against the floorboards and my starched skirt rustled with each step. As we approached the open doorway, I reached out for my stepmother's hand. Without looking, she batted my little hand away and reached into her black leather bag for another tissue.

The massive, shining wooden casket gleamed with polish and brass. The pungent perfume of a hundred flowers tickled my nostrils. I fought back a sneeze as I came to a halt, but a gloved hand in the small of my back nudged me along.

"Go on, Colleen, pay your respects to your father," my stepmother prompted.

I stumbled forward. The dread of seeing his still, gray face paralyzed my small body. My heart hammered in my chest. Alone, I dragged myself forward another step, then another.

I was trembling with terror.

Just as I reached the casket, I smelled the Old Spice aftershave that my father habitually wore, and I felt a deep sense of comfort as his presence surrounded me. I took another dragging step toward the spot where his body lay …

*   *   *

My eyelids fluttered as the warm, wet sensation slathered across my face. I rolled over and pulled the blankets up over my head.

"Bennie, ugh, go away! The sun is barely up."

My dog Bennie responded by snuffling his wet nose into the back of my neck. Giggling, I gave in and ruffled the big dog's ears. Truthfully, I was grateful to have been pulled out of the macabre dream of my father's untimely funeral. I had always been a prolific and vivid dreamer.

I sat up and pushed the hair flopping over my forehead out of my eyes. My hair was in an awkward in-between stage because I was in the middle of growing it out from the short cut I had worn for years. I had lots of headbands and barrettes stashed everywhere.

I rolled over, peeling the blankets back. I glanced at my dresser, where the photo of my father rested in a simple black frame. His receding dark blond hair brushed back uncompromisingly from his high forehead. A wide smile crinkled the corners of his sparkling blue eyes.

He had me hoisted up over a sheet cake frosted with chocolate icing adorned with white roses. Four yellow candles burned above the yellow lettering with the message: "Happy Birthday Colin!" The cake decorator at the Fresh Stop had not been on their game that day.

Regardless, I still loved the photo because my father was so happy, laughing at the misspelled cake and gazing at me with so much love and pride. The picture always made me smile.

I had regularly been able to sense my father's presence after he died. Not in an overt way, like seeing him sitting on the end of my bed, but more like an inner knowing that he was near. I would talk to him a lot when I was growing up and had always felt that he was listening. Sometimes, if I was able to focus intently, I could sense the nudge of guidance from him, which was a great comfort to me.

After I confessed my talks with my dad to my third grade best friend, Lilly Alvarez, I learned pretty quickly to shut down and tell no one else. Lilly thought it was strange that I spoke with a dead man, and she immediately activated the story on the Pinewood Elementary gossip network. Before you could say "boo," I was being made fun of as the "Miss Cleo" of the third grade. That's when I started eating lunch alone in the library.

I rolled over with a mighty sigh. Bennie's brown eyes were hopeful and his tail wagged tentatively. "Okay, boy, you win. Let's get your breakfast." I slipped into my beloved and well worn pale blue house slippers and stretched my arms overhead. "Let's go find everybody else."

I meandered toward the kitchen of my little house and was greeted by a miniature herd of animals. Henley and Mac, my other two dogs, along with my gray tabby cats, Lemon and Lime, all crammed into the hallway, joyfully mewing and huffing. With five animals weaving around my legs, trying to navigate around the moving boxes piled up all along the walls felt like an obstacle course.

I stood there for a moment and yawned, glancing at the clock on the kitchen wall. Waking up without setting an alarm was a privilege that I was still getting used to. Ever since I had been identified as the last scion of the wealthy founding family of my hometown, my life had changed in wonderful and sometimes scary ways.

For one, I was able to quit my job as assistant manager of the Pet Palace. I had decided to go into business for myself and open an inn. I had hired the local handyman, Jared Baumgartner, to do renovations as well as oversee the contractors for the new things like the sauna and hot tub for the spa, and the dog grooming facilities. The renovations were nearly complete.

The glass paneled door that led out to the enclosed porch, or, as I liked to call it when I was feeling fancy, the sunroom, squeaked loudly as the stiff hinges protested. I grimaced as I pulled the door open. My shoulder hit the door frame with a thud and I struggled to maintain my footing as the animals crowded through the door around my legs.

"Guys, calm down," I admonished my furry crew. "You're not going to get fed if you knock me out, you know. After I feed all of you, I'm due to meet with Jared at the new property by 9:00. Nine is a nice number, don't you think? And upside down, it becomes a six, which is pretty cool when you think about it. It's almost like a double agent number in disguise."

Bennie's brown and white face shone up at me affectionately as his entire fuzzy body wriggled with excitement. In the brilliant beam of morning sunlight, stray hairs flew and floated around his stout body like a hairy halo. A mysterious mix of breeds had produced long legs, a wiry coat, a rather gruesome face, and lopsided ears, but a heart of pure gold.

I had always preferred the company of animals. Growing up as an only child with a lot of social anxiety and without a lot of friends, animals were my constant companions. Animals let me ramble on as much as I wanted to, and they never got impatient or judgmental. Unlike most humans, my pets never made me feel like they couldn't wait to get away from me. Instead, they welcomed me and enjoyed my company. They liked the sound of my voice, even if they usually didn't understand what I was saying.

I filled the various bowls with kibble and stood back as the crew dug in. The October sun rose higher over the horizon and bathed the room in a warm rose gold, lending an unexpected beauty to my daily task. I would miss this little house.

I took a moment to lean back against the wall of the house and bask in the tangerine radiance that surrounded me. I hugged myself, rubbing the goosebumps that rose on my arms. The chill of autumn was beginning to settle over Pinewood Corners.

Autumn had always been my favorite season, and the Harvest Happenings festival was the best one of the year, in my opinion. Higgins' orchards and pumpkin patch would be open for apple picking and fresh-pressed cider, donuts, corn mazes, and wagon rides. The MB Squared Bakery would have their infamous seasonal iced pumpkin pie swirl bread for sale. And of course, everyone in town looked forward to the most popular annual dance in town, the Harvest Moon Masquerade Ball. Not that I ever had a date, but what the heck? I still had fun attending with a handful of other single ladies in town.

I took a deep breath, filling my lungs with the crisp morning air, smiled, and thought, *Today is going to be a good day.*

*   *   *

I tucked my insulated travel mug into the holder on the center console and pulled the seatbelt taut across my chest and lap as I clicked it into place and settled in for the short drive to my new property. *My property. Mine.*

I was still in a state of shock over the amazing turn my life had taken in the past seven months. Prior to Valentine's Day, I had been an orphan with no family, few friends, and a job that I loved that paid abysmal wages. I was scraping by, but content enough. I did enjoy working at the Pet Palace, helping the customers and getting to see everyone's pets. And, if I were to be completely honest with myself, I had been too afraid to reach for anything more. What if I stumbled and fell and lost what little I had managed to acquire? The devil you know, and all that.

But now, I had been identified as the sole remaining member of the founding family of Pinewood Corners, through a previously lost descendant, and with that had come a surprise windfall of inheriting the family's remaining assets, including a 15 carat heart-shaped ruby necklace with diamonds, set in platinum. The necklace was securely on display in the town's history museum. I still had to pinch myself nearly every day to believe my life was real.

Today, I was driving in my new Toyota SUV to visit my very own property to oversee the progress of the restoration of the old McIntyre house that I had purchased. I had always dreamed of running my own business. I loved animals and I desperately longed for a connection with more people. What better business could I start than a bed and breakfast that catered to pet lovers like me? I had decided to call it the Harvest Moon Inn, in honor of my favorite season and my love of the moon and all its phases.

I planned on catering to my guests with homemade pet food and treats made on site. Alongside the salon, hot tub, sauna, and massage room for the human guests, I was having a doggy day spa constructed. The pups could receive pampering while their owners enjoyed treating themselves. I glanced at my reflection in the side mirror as I switched lanes. I was grinning. I couldn't seem to stop grinning these days.

As I pulled up to the light at Oak and Main, I grabbed my coffee and took a sip. A patrol car wrapped with the Wingate County Sheriff's logo pulled up next to me. Sheriff Weaver was at the wheel. I waved to him and he returned the greeting with a smile and a salute. The Sheriff's youngest son, Martin, had been instrumental in finding the lost ruby necklace and uncovering the story of the lost descendant of the founding family last Valentine's Day. Sheriff Weaver was still in the honeymoon phase with his new bride, Joanna Morten, a lovely woman who also happened to be the grandmother to one of the owners of my favorite local baked goods and coffee shop, the MB Squared Bakery.

The light turned green and the sheriff pulled through the intersection and sped off. I pulled through at a more sedate pace, lowering the windows a few inches to better enjoy the crisp morning air.

The sunlight danced in dappled lace patterns through the yellowing leaves of the oak trees lining the sides of the road that bore their name. On impulse, I made a quick turn onto Main and drove past the MB Squared Bakery. There were already customers lined up clear out the door. I smiled, happy for my friends Mikki and Michael, the owners of the bakery.

I had gotten to know them last Christmas during a holiday cookie bake off. My booth had been right next to Mikki's, and she had been very kind to me. Plus, her baked goods were off-the-charts delicious. Now that she had paired up with Michael Brandon, her top competitor in the bake off, she had found romance and a thriving business. I sighed to myself as I parked my SUV, and figured that even if I had no hope for the former, at least I could shoot for the latter when I opened my inn.

I queued up behind the last person in line, an older, well-dressed gentleman in an obviously expensive and perfectly fitted overcoat. He turned to acknowledge me with a smile, and we immediately recognized each other. Mayor Reese's brown eyes traveled up and down my inexpensive attire—my five-year-old jacket with stains on the cuffs, well-worn jeans, and scuffed Bargain Mart vinyl boots. I had never been into fashion; dressing up always made me feel like a pigeon in peacock feathers. I usually just stuck with my good old jeans and sweatshirts with boots or sneakers.

"Good morning, my dear Ms. Perkins. Lovely to see you on this fine day!"

"Hi, Mayor Reese. You look nice today," I replied, feeling slightly self-conscious about my outfit. In spite of being a newly minted heiress, I just didn't have the knowledge or the desire to go shopping at designer stores and outfit myself in expensive clothes.

"How is the restoration going? It will be so wonderful to see the old McIntyre property looking fine again after all these years. There's a lot of history in that building, you know."

"Yes, sir," I replied, "The restoration is almost done, at least to the point where I can start receiving guests. I'm sure that I'll continue to make improvements as we go along."

"How is Jared working out?" the Mayor inquired, raising one sleek gray eyebrow.

"Oh, he's been so great, I can't sing his praises high enough. He's been steady and reliable, and he knows so much about home repair and restoration. I don't think I would be nearly so close to opening now if not for Jared. I mean, I knew he was handy and great at maintenance, but I had no idea that he knew how to match old wood stains with the heritage colors, and how to do carpentry and plumbing, and even electrical. Electricity scares me! I mean, you know, not like lamps and things, but the actual wiring, like, in the walls. That can be really dangerous, because …" I trailed off as I realized, too late, that Mayor Reese's eyes had taken on a glazed-over look that I was all too familiar with in the people I was speaking to. "Um, he's been just great," I finished lamely with a weak smile.

"I'm glad to hear it." Mayor Reese nodded curtly and turned his attention to the line in front of him, which had begun inching forward.

I pretended to check my phone, even though I hadn't heard it go off. To my surprise, I had a new text message from Mikki.

Hey, there! Come around the back, Michael has a flat white with your name on it.

I grinned and excused myself to Mayor Reese and headed around the bright white brick building toward the rear door. Said door was open, and a breathtakingly gorgeous man leaned on the doorframe, holding a green and white paper cup with the bakery's logo on the side. He saw me and smiled, going from handsome to ethereal. No doubt about it, my friend Mikki had snagged herself a very hot boyfriend.

"Morning, Michael." I pointed to the cup. "Is that for me?" I had coffee in the car, but it was not nearly as delicious as Michael's coffee.

Michael held the cup up in a salute. "Hey, gorgeous! Large flat white, with steamed oat milk, just the way you like it. If you're hungry, Mikki baked up a batch of her famous, award-winning cardamom cookies."

I broke into a trot. Those cookies always sold out within hours. Michael's partner, Mikki, had won runner-up in a recent holiday cookie baking championship with those melt-in-your-mouth orange and cardamom cookies dipped in dark chocolate. The very thought of them made my mouth water.

Michael laughed and said, "Hey, slow down, we set aside a dozen for you." I accepted the coffee and took a sip, sighing with appreciation. Michael's barista skills were as divine as his baking talents. Michael beckoned me to follow as he headed into the kitchen through the back door.

"Wow, what did I do to deserve this VIP treatment? Even Mayor Reese is waiting in line!"

"Mayor Reese likes to pretend he's 'one of the people' waiting in line in his $2,500 overcoat," Michael replied with a wink. "Politicians. Who knows why they think the way they do?"

Before I could reply, a petite brunette with flour on the tip of her nose and chocolate smeared on the bib of her apron popped through the doorway from the front and shrieked with delight.

"Colleen! How are you?" Mikki Branson ran to me and threw her arms around me, squeezing me tightly. I clutched my coffee, almost crushing the cardboard cup in an attempt to hang onto it without spilling it under the onslaught of Mikki's enthusiastic greeting.

"Hey, Mikki, good to see you. Business is booming!"

Mikki released her grip and stepped back. Her hazel eyes sparkled.

"Yes, it's been lines out the door all day long, until we run out of everything. I can't imagine what it's going to be like once the Harvest Happenings festival is in full swing." She blew a piece of her fine light brown hair out of her face. "Not that I'm complaining, it's a wonderful problem to have."

"Here, honey, put your hat on," Michael suggested, handing Mikki a white ball cap with the bakery's green MB Squared logo on the front.

Mikki tugged the hat on, tucking her hair back as she did so. "I'd better get back out there. I can't leave poor Melissa on her own for too long with that crowd." She grabbed a white baker's box from the metal table nearby and thrust it into my empty hand. "Here you go, I know they're your favorite. Enjoy! And we need to get together soon. I want to hear all about the restoration!" With a quick kiss to Michael's cheek, she was gone.

As I observed the look of love and admiration tinged with longing that Michael gave to Mikki's retreating form, I felt a stab of strong emotion. Was it jealousy? While I found Michael to be extremely attractive—most women would—I certainly had no romantic feelings toward him. Never mind that he was the boyfriend of one of my best friends—I just wasn't the type of woman to interest a man like Michael. I knew my limits.

The last man to truly care about me was my father, and he had died in a car accident when I was six. I had only had one sort-of boyfriend in my life, back in high school. He was a transfer student, rather chubby and shy with large glasses and a lisp, and we went to the movies twice and to one awkward homecoming dance before he transferred away. His father was involved in some sort of government job, and the family moved a lot.

Since then, nobody had been interested in pursuing a relationship with me, and I had learned to be content with my own company and a few close friends, as well as the companionship of my animals. Or so I had thought.

I realized that the sharp spike of feeling that I had from watching Michael look at Mikki with such obvious adoration really was jealousy, but not because I wanted Michael for myself. Rather, I wanted, deep down, what the two of them had together. What was prompting these feelings? Maybe I'd been reading too many spicy romance novels lately.

*   *   *

I took a moment to just sit in my vehicle and stare at the house. The sunlight gleamed on the freshly painted white belvedere rising above the dark gray roof shingles. Ornamental brackets typical of Italianate architecture adorned the tall, rectangular windows. Red brick walls contrasted beautifully with the black lacquered decorative shutters and white window frames. A wide row of stairs led to the front porch supported by square columns. A pair of glass-paneled doors opened to the front parlor, which would now serve as the lobby and check-in area.

The house had originally been built by one Ezra McIntyre in 1868. Ezra had made his fortune in the railroads, as many did in that time, but he was ready to settle down and start a family. Once his home was completed, he courted and married a woman—a girl, really, barely 17—named Delia. Ezra and Delia settled into the house and it was assumed that they lived happily for approximately two years, until Delia died giving birth to their first child, a stillborn boy. It was rumored that she had suffered several miscarriages prior to that, but back in those days, it wasn't proper to speak of such things, so there was no way to know if the rumors were true.

After Delia's passing, Ezra was distraught. He stopped attending social functions, even church services, fired all of his servants, and isolated himself completely. Neighbors had continued trying to help, regularly leaving food on his porch for him. One day, it was noticed that the food had not been brought inside and had piled up in front of the door, collecting flies. A party of local men was delegated to go to the house and investigate. As usual, their knocking was not answered, so the men broke the door down to discover poor Ezra hanging from the railings of the upper landing on the grand staircase.

Over the years, the building had been occupied occasionally, but never for long. It was boarded up after Ezra McIntyre's body was buried in Pinewood Cemetery beside his wife and son, and Pinewood Corners went on about its business as the years passed.

In the early 1900s, a steel baron named Walter Ellis had wanted a quieter life, so he bought the McIntyre house and moved his family in—a wife and three daughters. The stories told that the eldest daughter was jilted at the altar by her fiance and subsequently met the same fate as Ezra on the staircase. Convinced that the home was cursed, Walter Ellis abandoned the property and whisked his wife and younger daughters back to Pittsburgh as quickly as he could.

Rumors of hauntings and whispers of curses kept the house empty for decades. In the 1960s, a bunch of flower child hippies had invaded the property, squatting in their commune of free love and freely indulging in mind-altering substances, until the sheriff managed to evict them. The hippies had not complained of any hauntings, but perhaps their visions had a more logical explanation.

A married couple had tried their hand at opening a bed and breakfast in the house in the 1980s but their young son had vanished in the woods behind the property and had never been found. Overwhelmed by crippling grief, they closed up shop and moved out, leaving the place to the elements and vandals.

I didn't believe in curses or ghosts or any of that sort of thing. I had loved the house my whole life and used to go out of my way to walk past it on my way to school. It was almost like the house called out to me. My romanticized eyes had always seen the underlying beauty of the architecture and what the house once was and could be again—and not the sad ruin it actually was. I was thrilled to be able to bring it back to its potential shining glory.

My heart swelled with pride as I got out of the car, juggling the box of cookies and my cup of coffee. I climbed the porch stairs and headed for the front doors, assuming that Jared was inside and had left them unlocked.

"Morning." A deep, unfamiliar voice emanated from the dim far corner of the porch. I shrieked and fumbled the box of cookies. A man emerged from the shadows wearing a polo and khakis and carrying a briefcase. He was short and wiry, and he looked less like a threat and more like a businessman.

"I'm sorry if I startled you," he said, "You're Colleen Perkins, right?"

I nodded mutely and he continued.

"We had an appointment this morning to discuss your booking software. I'm Chad Aaronson, with Guestserve." He held out his right hand. I looked helplessly at the bakery box in one of my hands and the coffee in the other.

Chad quickly dropped his hand and asked if he could help me carry something. I politely declined and at that moment the front doors flew open and Jared Baumgartner, my handyman extraordinaire, scowled at the newcomer.

"You okay, Colleen? I thought I heard you screaming," he said. His beard bristled and his dark brown eyes blazed under his heavy brows.

"I'm okay, Jared, thanks. This is Mr. Aaronson, with the booking software company." I tipped my head toward the salesman. "We had a meeting scheduled this morning that I forgot. I guess I've had a lot going on, and I made an unplanned stop at the bakery. They gave me some cookies, and Michael, the owner, made me a flat white—those are my favorite—and it would've taken even longer but they let me come around back because I'm a friend, and—"

"Please, call me Chad," the man insisted, stepping forward to shake Jared's hand and effectively cutting off my monologue.

"Jared here has been helping me fix the place up," I explained, my cheeks reddening. "Won't you come in, and we can discuss your services."

*   *   *

An hour later, I had signed a contract and was on track to have my online booking services started. The system sounded good. I could now receive online bookings, manage dates that I wanted to make available or unavailable, and the guests who booked a reservation would receive an automatic email confirmation at the time of booking, as well as reminder emails a week before their reservation date. The software also allowed booking for pet grooming or spa services. Mentally checking off that item on my seemingly endless to-do list, I was about to go looking for Jared to get an update on what was left to be done for the day when there was a strident pounding on the front doors.

Curious to see who was knocking with such zeal, I hurried to answer. My heart fell as I saw Rayna Reese on my doorstep. Rayna was the Mayor's only daughter, and she was widely considered the most beautiful woman in Wingate County, with her long raven-black hair and wide violet eyes. Her amazing figure, delicate bone structure, smooth complexion, and lush lips backed up this claim, but unfortunately, her grating personality detracted from her beauty. Rayna ran the local newspaper, the *Pinewood Courier*. She was a terrible reporter, but her father owned the paper, so we had to put up with her purple prose and misspelled words.

I pasted on a smile. "Rayna, how nice to see you." I lied. "What can I do for you today?"

"I want to book a room. I have to review your new facility for the paper," Rayna replied in clipped tones. I noticed the two large rolling suitcases and the big carry on style tote, all matching in designer logos.

"I'm sorry, Rayna, but we won't be open to receive guests for at least another week. I haven't firmed up hiring a cook or housekeepers and don't even *ask* me about the difficulties of finding licensed spa technicians willing to work in a small town like this. I just got my booking software settled, and then I need to have a final inspection to make sure everything is good to go—for insurance reasons, you know, and then—"

"I want to book a room now. I assumed that you would have a preview for reporters, bloggers, influencers, and the like?" Rayna coolly interrupted me.

"Uh," I said, speechless for once.

Chapter 2

"Now, I don't want to go on record agreeing with Rayna Reese of all people, but you've got to admit that it's a smart idea," Jared remarked over cookies after I had finally convinced Ranya to leave, promising her that I would be able to accommodate her request in two weeks. Now I was seated with Jared on a cozy settee in one of the front parlors of the home.

"I suppose so." I sighed and reached for another cookie from the box on the coffee table. I could never resist sweets, hence my exaggerated waistline. "I could run ads and post on the inn's website that we're doing a soft opening for people who write reviews for new places like this. Maybe offer a reduced rate or something."

I picked at the label on my paper coffee cup. "But where am I going to find the rest of my employees? I need at least one more housekeeper—Eugenia Higgins can't handle it seven days a week, for goodness' sake—and a cook. Thankfully, Mikki and Michael have agreed to supply baked goods for continental breakfasts, and Michael showed me how to use that fancy espresso machine I bought, but if anyone wants something besides bread or pastry, I can't provide that, and I wanted to serve decent meals here. Not to mention, I need a cook willing to also fix dog-friendly food and treats! And I've been talking to a licensed massage therapist from Westbrook who might be willing to come three days a week, but I'm still looking for an aesthetician and a dog groomer, and I would love to find a manicurist if possible, so people can get a mani-pedi while someone else is having a facial or a massage. Oh no, what if a couple wants a couples massage? I would need *two* massage therapists." I finally ran out of breath as my stomach churned.

Jared wiped his hands on a napkin. "Can't please everybody all of the time." He rose, dusted the front of his faded dark blue work shirt, and tossed the crumpled napkin into the nearby trash can. "Listen, my brother, Brett, is a lawyer. He's the smart one in the family. I can ask him to draw up some boilerplate employment contracts for you, if you want," Jared offered. "And I may know a few people who know a few people who are looking for jobs."

I was about to protest that I couldn't afford an attorney, but then I remembered that I could. It was odd, recalling that I was now a wealthy woman. Grinding paycheck to paycheck for most of my life had become a habit that was mentally hard to break.

I swallowed my discomfort and said, "Well, if it helps things along, I can offer a good hourly rate, and even a small bonus if I can find folks willing to start by the beginning of next week, if you think that will help find some employees quickly. I can't run this place alone, and the last thing I need is to have Rayna writing reviews that say my inn has poor service and no amenities!" Stricken, I reached for another cookie and shoved half of it into my mouth. "Besides," I mumbled through a mouthful of cookie, crumbs flying, "I'm not a great cook, and I have no training or certification in any spa treatments. Goodness knows why I thought I could pull something like this off." My eyes were wide with trepidation.

Jared calmly strode over, the tread of his heavy boots loud on the floorboards, and gently patted my shoulder.

"You've had plenty of sugar and caffeine this morning. What you need is some chamomile tea, maybe a sandwich. I'll fix you right up." He turned and disappeared through the doorway toward the kitchen. I could hear him rattling around, slamming cabinets and running water. I concentrated on taking slow, deep breaths in an effort to calm myself down.

The sheer amount of things I had to do was overwhelming. I would be moving into the house myself next week. I would eventually be living in the groundskeeper's cottage at the rear of the property, but it was in a state of exceptional disrepair and wouldn't be inhabitable for several more months, so I would be staying temporarily in one of the smaller bedrooms on the second floor.

I grabbed my phone and opened my notes app and typed *hire movers* on one of my many to-do lists. Thankfully, most of the dreadful administrative tasks, like getting my permits and licenses and such had been taken care of long ago. My friend Lacey, the head librarian of the Pinewood Corners library, had been an enormous help to me with all of that stuff.

It had been Lacey who had found the online course in hospitality management that I had taken over the past summer. It was essentially a crash course in how to run my inn effectively, and I was grateful to have had the experience. Without the course to help me feel more prepared—and without the necessary escape offered by the risque romance novels from the library that I eagerly consumed—I would have probably collapsed from anxiety by now.

Just as I was closing the notes app and getting ready to set down my phone, Jared entered the room carrying a tray. He set the tray on the coffee table. I saw a steaming pot of what I assumed to be tea, two delicate china cups, and two sandwiches on separate small china plates.

I had gone around to all the thrift stores and antique shops in Pinewood Corners and the surrounding areas, and exhaustively searched websites like Ebay, and had managed to cobble together an eclectic collection of dishes and glassware that were either early to mid-20th century or were reasonable facsimiles.

I had also found much of the furniture and decor pieces and artwork during my foraging trips and online searches. Luckily, the attic had produced several good pieces, including multiple massive oak and walnut bedsteads with matching wardrobes and a large dining table and chairs that only needed a fresh coat of stain and polish. I was amazed that the furniture had survived up there through all the years the house had been abandoned. I supposed that the rumors of the house being haunted had been good for keeping curious people out.

I leaned forward, gesturing for Jared to sit, and carefully poured the tea. The golden liquid filled the cups as the soothing floral apple scent of the chamomile wafted through the room. I chose a plate for myself and bit into the sandwich. It was chicken salad, studded with dried cranberries and walnuts, redolent with herbs. "Jared, this sandwich is delicious! Did you make the chicken salad?"

He blushed, I think. It was hard to see what was going on between Jared's beard and mustache, along with his heavy brows and the bangs of his dark blond bowl cut laying low across his forehead. But the two inches of cheeks I could see definitely looked redder than usual.

"It wasn't too hard," he said. "I had picked up a rotisserie chicken at the Fresh Stop for dinner last night. I had plenty extra so I just mixed up some chicken salad that I brought with me today. It's great to have a batch on hand for lunches." He waved off my compliments and took a large bite of his own sandwich.

"Hey, maybe you should be my cook," I teased. The patches of Jared's visible facial skin became even redder. "I'm just kidding. You're a fantastic handyman, I wouldn't want to split your focus. Can you even imagine? Clogged toilet in the Honeymoon Suite, after you finish making lunch." I chuckled then sobered. "Oh my goodness, I'm acting like you'll be working here full time after we open. I'm sure you have lots of clients waiting for your services. I know I'm excited to finally have my own service, and you've had your own handyman business for years. I wouldn't dream of taking you away from that, or trying to, I mean." My throat suddenly felt dry and I sipped my tea.

Jared surprised me by laughing heartily. "That would be a sight, all right. Me, in a frilly apron, making sandwiches with the crusts cut off for the fancy guests at your inn."

"Hey, the apron is entirely optional," I teased him, "but hairnets are mandatory—including the ones that cover your beard." I burst out laughing at the mental image of sturdy Jared in a hairnet and beard net, and he joined in with his own warm chuckle at the thought.

After a moment, Jared said, "I do enjoy working here. It's been fulfilling to see the old place come back to life. This house has good bones. It just needed some TLC and some hope."

I tipped my head to the side. "Hope? What do you mean?"

"You know all the stories about this place; you've lived here in Pinewood Corners all your life like I have. My thinking is that when so much darkness invades a house, it needs a good dose of hope to bring the light back."

"Why, Jared, that's beautiful. Do you believe all the stories?"

Jared scratched his head with one calloused finger. "The historical part of the stories, sure. The people that lived here and died here, there's records of all that. You can ask Martin Weaver, he volunteers at the historical society. You can research and prove that part. The rest of the stories, the curse and the restless spirits …" He hesitated a moment, and looked around, eyes darting as if checking for potential eavesdroppers. His voice lowered almost to a whisper, he leaned forward and continued. "I don't know about all that, but in the months that I've been here, I've heard some things and seen some things that make me wonder."

Icy fingers trailed down my back as I shuddered. "What sort of things?" I demanded.

Jared shook his large, round head. "I don't want to frighten you, and I don't want to influence you."

"Influence me?"

"Like if I said that I had seen a lady in a blue gown in the kitchen, then you might unconsciously be influenced to see something similar, simply because I planted the idea in your mind by telling you that." He added, "Not that I've seen a lady in blue in the kitchen, or anywhere else for that matter."

I tapped my chin. "No, I see what you mean. If either of us experiences anything paranormal—" I noticed Jared flinched at the word. "If we see or hear anything unusual, then we should independently write it down, keep a record, then maybe compare notes. That way we can remain unbiased by one another."

Jared nodded thoughtfully. "Makes sense," he said. We finished the rest of our lunch in companionable silence.

*   *   *

The next morning, Jared arrived at the inn bright and early, brandishing a pocket-sized notebook and pen. "For recording any weird stuff, like you suggested," he explained. He also provided me with a list of names and phone numbers of people he knew of that were looking for work or open to finding a new position.

"Thanks! Do you happen to know any movers?" I asked.

"Yeah, my cousin Sammy and his buddies would be glad to help you move your stuff for a cooler full of soda and a couple of pizzas."

I laughed. "I can provide that, along with a fair wage, if you're serious."

"Sure, I'll give Sammy a call. When do you need him?"

We worked out the details, and my cell phone began to ring.

"Hello?" I answered.

"Ms. Perkins?" a pleasant male voice asked. "This is Brett Baumgartner. I'm Jared's brother. He asked me to give you a call. He said you might need some simple employment contracts drawn up?"

"Oh. Oh, yes," I responded. Why was it that I could talk until I was hoarse about nothing at the most inappropriate times, but when I wanted to respond intelligently, I froze like a squirrel being stalked by a bobcat?

"Well, I'm happy to help you out with that," Brett assured me. After a brief consultation, we made an appointment for the following afternoon to meet in person, and I turned my attention to calling the numbers that Jared had supplied and setting up interviews with the people on the list of potential employees that Jared had provided.

Several hours later, I was seated in the front east parlor across from Sandy Wilcox. Sandy was new to Pinewood Corners. She had long dark hair that hung very straight over her shoulders and down her back. Her snapping dark brown eyes shone from her olive complexion. She and her husband had moved to town so that her husband could realize his dream of opening a glass blowing studio and gallery. Sandy explained that while her husband was extremely talented, it would take a while for the business to get going and make a profit, so she wanted to contribute an income until their business could sustain them.

"Rick thinks that Pinewood Corners is a real up-and-coming artisan town, what with all the festivals getting so popular and attracting so many visitors and drawing new businesses, especially after that lady inherited that lost necklace," Sandy informed me. "Lots of people come to town to see that necklace in the historical society museum. I went and saw it myself, right after we arrived in town. It's amazing!"

My eyes widened and my hand flew to my chest. "Oh, I'm that lady! I mean, I'm the one who inherited the necklace and everything. That's what enabled me to buy and renovate the house and start this business. I loved the job I was doing; I worked for the Pet Palace for years. I love animals, I felt almost guilty about leaving, but how could I let my dreams go?"

Sandy looked impressed. "Well, I love this house. I think I can clean and change bed linens for you, and I would love to work here."

I consulted her application again. I was a little worried in the back of my mind that she would soon quit if her husband's studio took off, but if I was going to be hesitant to hire some-one simply because they might quit, I wouldn't be doing much hiring.

"Well, Sandy, I might be going out on a limb here, but I'm going to offer you a job. Four days a week." I named a salary that Brett had suggested as more than reasonable, and Sandy beamed and shook my hand.

"Thanks, Ms. Perkins, you won't regret it."

"I'll have my lawyer draw up the paperwork for you to sign later today, so keep an eye on your email," I told her as I walked her to the front doors.

I felt like things were finally falling into place as I watched Sandy make her way down the porch stairs. With a satisfied sigh, I turned to head for the kitchen when my cell phone vibrated in my pocket as my ringtone echoed through the foyer. I glanced at the screen and noted a local number and swiped on the green button to answer.

"Ms. Perkins? This is Leah Miller. I got a call from you about a job?"

"Yes, Jared Baumgartner thought you might be inter-ested in a position here at the Harvest Moon Inn. He said that you're a skilled dog groomer, and—"

"The McIntyre place? You can't be serious, Everyone knows that place is haunted. I wouldn't set foot in that place if you offered me the McKinney necklace! No, thank you!"

My phone beeped as she hung up on me. I stood blinking, stunned at Leah's emphatic reaction. I pulled the list of poten-tial employees out of my pocket, smoothed it out, and studied it again. Clearly I was having better luck with folks who were new in town and didn't know the history and rumors about the house. I placed one hand on the wall. I fancied that I could feel the vibrations of the house itself pulsing, and I raised my eyes to the ceiling. "I really need to find people to hire and help me run this place smoothly and make it a success. Please, help me find people who will love you as much as I do," I murmured.

"What's that?" Jared appeared in the foyer from out of nowhere.

I jumped and cursed under my breath. "Jared, you scared the living daylights out of me," I gasped.

"I finished planing down the window sash in the yellow room," Jared said, "and I wanted to see how the job interviews were going."

"Not great, I'm one for two so far. Sandy Wilcox was happy to accept a housekeeping position, but Leah Miller was terrified of the house and hung up on me."

Jared shook his head, his dark blond hair flopping on his forehead. "Leah's always been too superstitious for her own good. I shouldn't have suggested that you call her. Try calling Betsy Killian, I heard she's unhappy at Puppies in Suds. She might be interested." With that, he turned and lumbered back the way he had come.

I did an online search for the number and called Puppies in Suds and asked for Betsy.

"Hello?" a breathless voice came on the line.

"Betsy, this is Colleen Perkins, from the Harvest Moon Inn. How are you?"

"I'm pretty busy at the moment, Colleen. I'm covering for two other employees right now, as usual, so what is it I can help you with?"

"I know this is wildly inappropriate, seeing as you're currently at work and all, but I'm looking for a dog groomer for my inn. I was wondering if you might be interested?"

"Let me call you back on my lunch hour." The line went dead. I couldn't decide if that was a good sign or not, since I hadn't had a chance to give Betsy my number.

I wandered into the kitchen so that I could make the remaining calls. I loved this room. Jared had expanded the kitchen and installed up-to-date appliances, including a huge double refrigerator and separate freezer, a cooktop with six burners and and a flat top griddle, two double ovens and an island with a prep sink in addition to the large farmhouse sink embedded in the granite countertops that lined the room. There was also a commercial-grade dishwasher under the counter next to the sink.

The tall windows let in lots of sunlight, and the breakfast table on the far end of the room and the copper-bottomed pots hanging from the wrought iron rack over the island gleamed. The walls were painted a lovely warm cream that contrasted nicely with the black cabinets and pot rack. I hoped that the cook I would hire soon would be happy preparing food for my guests here. The butler's pantry next to the breakfast table had been converted into a large walk-in pantry with lots of shelving and storage cabinets.

I settled down at the table with my list, an additional note-book, and my phone to start making calls. An hour later, I had arranged to meet with a potential cook, two people interested in the front desk position, and I had set up an online inter-view with a couple from the next town over. They were both licensed aestheticians and massage therapists. They had expe-rience running a spa and sounded very interested in running mine. Pleased at my progress, I rose from the table and heard the door chimes peal.

Fervently hoping it wasn't Rayna again, I made my way to the front door. It turned out to be Betsy Killian, from the dog grooming salon. Betsy was petite with watery pale blue eyes and candy-floss fine platinum blonde hair that floated around her head like a halo.

I quickly learned that she was frustrated with being relied upon to cover for lax employees at her current job, without the benefit of any extra pay. She was thrilled to accept my job offer. After I had shown her around the newly built pet spa area and named a salary that was higher than what she cur-rently made, she was even more excited to get to work.

"This is such a perfect opportunity. I'll go back to Puppies in Suds right now and put in my notice so that I can start when you're ready to open!" Betsy shook my hand enthusiastically. Betsy seemed to have no concerns about the rumors surround-ing the house. If only my other interviews would go so well.

After Betsy left, I was excited to tell Jared about my new employee and went in search of him. I made my way toward the main staircase and heard the unmistakable sound of weeping.

"Jared?" I called and waited. No answer, just the soft weeping, as if someone had received the most devastating news and had completely broken down. "Jared?" I repeated, pitching my voice louder as I began hurrying up the stairs. The weeping sounded distinctly female. Who else was in my house?

Chapter 3

My feet moved faster than my brain as I rushed up the staircase and down the upstairs hallway.

"Oof!" I cried out as my face was momentarily embedded in flannel. I bounced off Jared's chest and stumbled backwards. Jared reached out and caught me by the shoulders.

"Colleen, are you okay? What happened?" His brown eyes radiated concern.

"I was looking for you, and then out of nowhere, I thought that I heard—"

Jared held up a work-roughened hand to stop my flow of speech. He reached into his pocket and waved his little notebook in the air. "Write it down, don't tell me."

I didn't have a notebook on me, so I pulled my phone out of my jeans pocket and tapped my experience into the notes app.

Jared seemed satisfied. "Now, we switch and see what the other wrote," he explained, holding out his small red notebook. I took it, and handed him my phone with the note on display.

I flipped to the first page and saw today's date at the top. In Jared's neat and compact printing were the words *The weeping lady is back today. I have heard her several times before, and I have not seen her but I have felt some cold spots on the stairs. She is always heard on or near the stairs. She sounds very sad.*

Okay, it wasn't Shakespeare, but it got the point across. I felt the hairs on my arms stand at attention as a chill vibrated through my body.

Jared's hand felt cold when it brushed mine as we exchanged the notebook and phone again.

"It looks like we heard the same thing," he remarked.

I tried to swallow but my throat was dry. It was hard to describe how I felt. I didn't feel afraid, necessarily. It was more of a feeling of deep sadness, as if I could tune into the emotions of the weeping woman. I suddenly felt like an empty container with sorrow pouring in and filling me up to overflowing. I took a deep breath and mentally cut off the feeling before it could overtake me completely.

"Well, I feel sorry for her, whoever she is," I said brusquely.

"What should we do?" Jared asked.

"Do?" My eyes widened. "What do you mean?"

"I mean, do we get someone in here to exorcize the ghost?"

I felt a huge wall of resistance rise up from the center of my chest. "Jared Baumgartner, you will do no such thing. This is that spirit's home. We can't kick her out!"

"But what if she's stuck? What if she wants to move on but she can't?"

I threw up my hands. "Why are we even discussing this as if it were a rational problem with a rational solution? It could be anything, or nothing. Maybe it's bad plumbing or something. Let's just keep going forward as we've been doing, getting ready for opening day." Determined to shove the memory of the feelings from the weeping spirit out of my mind, I turned and stomped back down the stairs, leaving Jared staring after me in the hallway.

*   *   *

By the end of the week, I had hired the couple, George and Lisa Hall, to run my spa, and a lovely widow named Mrs. Blake to cook meals, as well as Betsy the dog groomer. I also hired two girls who were students at the local community college to work shifts at the front desk. The inn had passed inspection with flying colors. Things were rolling along. I had put the word out on my website and through a couple of well-placed ads that the soft opening—for industry professionals and those in the media—would be in one week. I was in the process of moving most of my things into storage temporarily while I stayed in the second floor bedroom. My animals would be with me, of course.

Making his way to the front door, Sammy, Jared's cousin asked, "Anything else, Ms. Perkins?" He was a hard worker, and he and his buddies had moved everything in no time.

"No, not right now, Sammy, but I may want some help in the future when I move into the groundskeepers cottage. It's on the property, just at the back. I had some fears that I would need to live in the house, in case one of my guests needs something in the night, but then Jared reminded me that I can always set up a phone line direct to my house from the front desk so the guests can reach me twenty-four hours a day. I can even have the calls forwarded to my cell if I happen to be out for any reason, and I do intend to hire another manager eventually."

"Sure thing, Ms. Perkins, just shoot me a text." Sammy grinned at my long-winded speech and gave Bennie a final pat before he left.

I was exhausted from all the moving and in desperate need of a shower and something to eat. As I was contemplating which need I should meet first, the door chimes rang out and my dogs responded by barking hysterically. Assuming that Sammy must have forgotten something, I pulled the door open without hesitation.

The caller was not Sammy. It was a man I had never seen before, with slicked back jet black wavy hair. He whipped off his mirrored aviator style sunglasses as soon as I opened the door. When he smiled, his high cheekbones accented the way his eyes crinkled attractively at the corners. His teeth were even and white. He tucked his sunglasses into an interior pocket of his fitted blazer and held out a hand.

"Hi, there, I'm Scott Carpenter. I'm a freelance travel writer and I saw your ad. I couldn't resist this charming place, so I hopped in the car and headed right over to book a room. I'm hoping to write an in-depth review of the Harvest Moon Inn that will sell to *Lodging Magazine* or perhaps even *Travel and Leisure.*" He gestured to a small fluffy white dog seated by his feet. "And this is Ranger. He gets along well with other animals," he added, peering around me at the trio of curious canines wagging behind me.

I stood there gaping, my hand like a dead fish in his, acutely aware of my grubby old clothes and the limp bandana covering my hair.

"Oh, well, we're not actually scheduled for the soft opening for almost a week, that's when all my employees start, so …" I trailed off, at an uncharacteristic loss for words.

"No worries, I saw a fantastic retro diner on my way through town, and several nice looking bakeries and coffee shops. If you've got a bed and bathroom, I'll be all set. No need to change the sheets every day. Ranger and I can look after ourselves." His eyes were a brilliant cobalt blue in contrast to his black hair and the shadow of black stubble scattered evenly over his square jaw.

Holy smokes, he's gorgeous. He could be a model.

"The El," I replied cryptically, still mesmerized.

"I'm sorry?" the man, Scott, asked. He pulled a pair of black-framed glasses out of his jacket pocket and slipped them on. *Mmmm, Clark Kent vibes, yummy!*

I shook myself mentally and tried to get a grip on my runaway thoughts. "I mean the diner. It's called the El Royale, but we locals refer to the restaurant as the El. It's a great place to eat."

"Great, can I book a room, then?"

"I—uh—" I sensed movement out of the corner of my eye as Jared entered the room. He looked from me to the newcomer.

"Hi, I'm Jared. I help run the place," he stated. I made no move to correct him.

"This is Scott, um, and he's a travel writer and he wants to book a room now, but we're not ready yet."

"Scott Carpenter," the man supplied, shaking hands with Jared. "I love this house. It's so quaint. And the building has quite the history. I headed down as soon as I saw the ad and did a little research on the place. I wanted to be sure to secure a room immediately so that I can scoop all the other writers."

Jared narrowed his eyes. "Why didn't you book online?"

"The site won't allow anyone to make reservations before next week, so I thought I could come here in person and check in," Scott replied smoothly. "The fact that this is a pet-friendly establishment sealed the deal for me."

"Well, I suppose we can accommodate that, if you're not expecting any gourmet meals before next week. I could put you and Ranger in the blue room."

I had decorated each guest room in a dominant color that also served as the name for the room for identification purposes.

"That would be so great, thank you," Scott beamed.

After I checked Scott in, Jared showed him to his room. When Jared returned alone, I asked him about the new guest.

"He said he's going to change and freshen up, get his dog settled and then go to dinner," Jared told me. "You want me to stay here tonight? I don't know if you should be alone with him here."

"Don't be silly, I'm bound to be alone with male guests when I run an inn. Besides, he seems perfectly nice."

Jared grunted in reply and then mumbled something so quietly that I didn't understand him. I asked him to repeat what he had said.

Changing the subject, he said, "I have a surprise for you." Then he gestured for me to follow him as he headed toward the front door.

Curious, I followed. He led me down the front path to the sidewalk. Then he stopped, turned, and pointed.

Planted on the dying autumn lawn in the setting sun, surrounded by a handful of fallen leaves, was a wooden sign suspended from a wrought iron frame. It was painted in black lacquer to match the house's shutters and accents and it proclaimed in golden letters matching the font from my website and stationary and brochures "Harvest Moon Inn, est. 2024." In smaller letters along the bottom, I saw the words "Colleen Perkins, Proprietor." The phone number and website appeared below that. Tears filled my eyes as I turned and threw my arms around a very startled Jared.

"Thank you! It's beautiful! The perfect finishing touch." I squeezed him and let go.

"Oh, it was nothing, I wanted to make sure it was done before your official opening." Jared waved off my praises in his humble way and lumbered back to the house.

I remained on the lawn, staring at my new sign. My eyes were drawn to a movement in an upstairs window when I caught sight of a curtain being drawn back. A figure stood in silhouette, looking down at me. I figured it was my new guest and shrugged it off as the curtain fell back into place.

The front doors opened and Scott Carpenter emerged wearing dark washed jeans and a black pullover sweater that made his blue eyes pop. He paused on the porch, taking in the rocking chairs and suspended swing.

The planter boxes and hanging baskets would be bursting with flowers come springtime, but for now, I had orange and black trick-or-treat pansies in the boxes as well as pots of yellow and orange mums lining the stairs. The vibes were definitely on point for the Halloween season.

"Mind if I take a few photos while the sun's still up?" he called out to me.

"Sure, go for it," I told him. I expected him to whip out his cell phone camera, but he surprised me by producing an actual digital camera—and a nice one too, from the looks of it. He snapped several photos from various angles on the porch, and then strolled down to join me on the lawn. He raised the camera and took some shots of the front of the building with the rosy rays of the setting sun reflecting off the windows.

"Hey, were you looking out one of the front windows upstairs right before you came outside?" I asked him.

He looked puzzled. "No, my room is at the back of the house. I changed and came straight down. Why?"

I shook my head. "No reason." I waved him off and told myself that the sunlight reflecting off the window panes must have been playing tricks on my eyes.

"Since I'm new to town, I could use a friendly guide to show me around," he said. When I didn't respond, he said,

"Have dinner with me, and tell me all about how you found this wonderful house."

I automatically reached up and touched the bandanna. "Oh, I'm not fit to go out right now," I protested.

"Nonsense," Scott reached out and gently pulled my hand away from my head. To my stunned surprise, he then drew my hand to his lips and pressed a kiss to the back of it. "I love a self-deprecating woman. You look absolutely perfect for a retro diner."

"Well," I was absurdly flattered and hoped that the rosy sunset would hide my blush. "I guess I do look good enough for the El, anyway."

"Then you'll come to dinner with me?" Scott's eyes shone.

"Okay, sure, I'll go, what the heck. Just let me tell Jared."

"No need, I'm sure he'll figure it out. He seems like an intelligent fellow," Scott said as he placed a hand on the small of my back and began steering me toward a low-slung silver sedan parked across the way.

I tried to protest, because I didn't even have my purse, but Scott insisted that we go before I changed my mind and assured me that the meal was his treat. He escorted me around the car to the passenger side and opened the door for me, holding my elbow delicately as I climbed in. He got into the driver's seat and we were off. The interior of the car was oddly silent with no music playing.

"You'll want to turn left up ahead," I said.

"I remember where the restaurant is," Scott replied without taking his eyes off the road. His profile was stunning, with a chiseled jaw, full lips, and sloping nose under a strong brow.

We pulled into the parking lot of the diner within a few minutes. One of the perks of living in a small town was that everything was nearby. The lot was filled with cars and Scott had to circle a few times before he found someone backing out and took the vacated spot.

"Popular place," he remarked. "The food must be good."

"It is. It's nothing fancy, mind you, but good classic diner food, and the decor and ambiance are really great. The owner, Darlene, is a real character, too. She bought the place from the original owner a few years back, but she didn't change the place much. It's really neat inside, wait till you see," I rambled, nervous to enter the diner with him, afraid people would make a fuss and embarrass both of us, but more afraid that I would make a fool of myself.

Wordlessly, Scott got out of the car. I opened my door and there he was, ready to help me with his hand outstretched. I placed my clammy hand in his and hauled myself very ungracefully out of the low seat of the car. Tucking my hand into the crook of his elbow, Scott sauntered toward the diner's front door. As we approached, the guitar solo from Pat Benatar's "Hit Me with Your Best Shot" blasted out of the doors.

The El Royale diner was a fixture in Pinewood Corners. It was decorated in well-maintained original 1960s glitter-embedded vinyl booths and metal and formica tables and a matching bar. The jukebox had been updated through the 1980s and was always playing hits from Van Halen and Journey and the like. Scott held the door open and gestured for me to walk through. I took a deep breath and entered. My stomach growled at the wonderful scents of coffee and bacon, frying meat and toasting bread.

"Hi, welcome to the El. Would you like to sit at the bar or a table, or wait for a booth?" The smiling hostess addressed Scott. He looked at me questioningly, dark brows raised.

"Hi, Frannie," I said, and the girl seemed to notice me for the first time. "A table will be fine."

She grabbed two large laminated menus from the hostess stand and led us to a table for two. Scott's head swiveled around as we wound our way toward the table that Frannie indicated.

"This place is even better than I had imagined," he remarked with delight.

Scott insisted on pulling my chair out for me, and I had an awkward moment of pulling myself forward as he pushed the chair under me and I sat with a thud. *How do women normally do this?* It was a new experience for me. As Scott took his own seat, Frannie handed us the menus and I noticed that she placed a lingering hand on Scott's shoulder.

"You just give me a holler if you need anything else, okay?" She gave a squeeze to his shoulder and ran her hand over his bicep before she winked and sashayed away with an extra swing of her hips. I mentally rolled my eyes at what fools women tended to make of themselves in the presence of a half-decent looking man. *But Scott isn't half-decent looking, he's absolutely stunning.*

"Howdy, folks!" The friendly, booming voice broke me out of my thoughts and I looked up to see Darlene, the El's owner, standing next to the table. "My, my, my," she said, looking at Scott. "Colleen, I see you brought George Clooney's younger brother into the El," she joked.

"Darlene, this is Scott Carpenter. He's in town to stay at the inn and write an article about it."

Scott shook Darlene's hand. "Pleased to meet you," he said.

"Pleasure's all mine, darlin'," she beamed and pumped his hand vigorously. She popped her gum as she pulled an old-fashioned order pad from the pocket of her apron and extracted a pen from the depths of her platinum beehive hairstyle. No fancy electronic tablets at the El, they were old-school all the way. "What'll you have to drink?"

"I'll just have a Sprite," I said. Sprite was my favorite soda.

Scott studied the menu and his eyes lit up. "Don't tell me that you have cherry Coke floats!" he cried.

"Okay, I won't," Darlene teased, "I'll just bring you one!"

"This place is a true gem," Scott told her. "I may have to write a separate article all about your wonderful restaurant."

"In that case, sugar, your Coke float is on the house," Darlene winked, tucked the pen back behind her ear. "I'll be back with your drinks and to get your food orders," she said as she strolled away, her hips and her big plastic hoop earrings swinging in time with her easy gait.

Scott watched her walk away and shook his head in an admiring fashion. "I love this town. I've met so many interesting characters already." He leaned forward and met my eyes. "So tell me how you stumbled across your beautiful home."

Something about the way that Scott looked at me made me feel like I was the only person in the entire room and that he was hanging on every word that I said. I had never felt so seen before. For the first time in my life, my mouth dried up and I was entirely without words. I reached for the water glass in front of me to buy myself a few seconds of time. I sipped and held up one finger. Scott sat patiently, wordlessly encouraging me to speak.

"Well, I was born in Pinewood Corners, and the McIntyre mansion was always there. It was abandoned by the last owners back in the 1980s, and it was boarded up and in pretty bad shape. I used to walk by it on my way to and from school. I took the long way on purpose just to see it because I always loved the lines and the shape of the windows and how the belvedere rose up out of the roof. It always seemed like such a dignified house, and it could be so lovely if only someone would put a little—a lot—of love and care into it." I paused for another sip of water. "Long story short, I coveted that house from the time I was a little girl, and when I recently came into some money, I decided to make my dreams come true."

Scott sat back and whistled low and long. "Wow, that's awesome, you wanted it and you went out and got it, after a lifetime of admiring it."

I looked down and picked at my napkin. "It was a lot of luck, and a lot of things falling into place. Most folks probably think I'm crazy to try and make a go of it as an inn."

"Especially with all the stories about the curse and the hauntings," Scott said off-handedly.

I choked on my water. My eyes streamed as I coughed and fought for breath. Scott jumped up and ran around the table to pound me on the back.

"I'm okay," I rasped. "Went down the wrong pipe." I thudded my fist on my chest.

"I'm sorry if I was rude just then, I didn't mean to be. But the stories about the house are out there on the internet, and the deeds of the various owners are public record, as are the archived newspaper articles about them. I do my research before I stay at a place. It makes for a more well-rounded article."

Before I could respond, Darlene returned with our drinks and her order pad. "What'll it be, kids?" She stood with her pen poised over the paper.

"I'll have the veggie club with fries," I replied.

Scott studied the menu again. "I'm assuming the veggie club has no meat products?" he asked. "I'm a strict vegetarian."

"Oh my gosh, me too!" I cried. "Sometimes I feel like I'm the only one in town."

"Not anymore," Scott assured me. "I just love and respect animals too much to eat them. How about the portobello and Swiss burger and a side of coleslaw?"

"Coming right up, sugar," Darlene winked, revealing a lid covered with bright blue eyeshadow. I grinned from ear to ear, delighted to find something in common with Scott.

After Darlene left the table, Scott returned his laser focused attention to me. "Again, I apologize if I made you uncomfortable earlier. I'm sure you've heard all the stories, having grown up here and all."

"Of course," I replied, pausing to sip my soda.

"Do you believe?" Scott asked me. I didn't need to ask him what he meant. I played with the sugar packets on the table, pulling them out of their bowl and fanning them out in a circle on the table top, stalling for time to come up with a suitable answer.

"I don't know, maybe. I'm not convinced one way or another. I don't think anyone has the definitive answer to whether or not the spirits of the dead can be felt by the living."

Scott pursed his lips thoughtfully. "Interesting. Have you had any experiences personally?"

I didn't know why, but I was hesitant to tell him about the weeping lady that Jared and I had heard. It seemed like a personal moment with Jared and I wasn't comfortable revealing the experience to Scott without Jared there to tell his side of the story. I simply shrugged and said, "Not really, just the creaks and bangs associated with any older structure."

Scott looked disappointed. "I've heard that restorations often stir up paranormal activity. If you haven't seen or heard anything unusual, then your house probably doesn't have a very active haunting."

"But that's good, I don't want people afraid to stay at my inn!" I said.

"Would you believe that the Lizzie Borden house where the ax murders actually took place is now a bed and breakfast with a months-long waiting list? It's said to be very haunted, and plenty of people want to go there expressly to interact with spirits."

I looked up from my glass. Scott had whipped cream on his upper lip from his float. The cream mustache combined with his super-serious expression made laughter bubble up in my chest and I couldn't hold it in. "I'm sorry," I giggled, "you just look so funny with cream on your lip, talking so intently about the Lizzie Borden house." I wiped my eyes.

Scott smiled and handed me one of the napkins he had pulled out of the dispenser on the table. "Hey, I'll make a fool of myself any day to see you smile and laugh like that."

I held out a paper-wrapped straw. "Better use this," I told him. He accepted the straw, and our hands brushed briefly. I felt a distinct tingling sensation where our skin made contact. I shuddered, suddenly sobered.

"What is it? What's wrong?" Scott seemed attuned to my slightest change in mood.

"It's nothing, I'm just feeling a bit light-headed, I need to eat something."

Scott shoved the little bowl of wrapped saltines my way. "Here, have a cracker while we wait for our food."

Our food was delivered shortly and Scott ate every morsel. He proclaimed it the best portobello burger he'd had in a very long time. When Darlene asked if we wanted dessert, I declined, much to Scott's obvious disappointment.

"I've got something better in mind," I said, "Don't worry, I don't skip dessert—obviously." I gestured vaguely to my figure.

"Stop putting yourself down, you're a healthy and strong woman, own it," Scott admonished. "Not many people would take an inheritance and invest it in running a business. Most people would want to live a life of leisure, but you want to work hard and make a life for yourself and your family. That's admirable."

"I don't really have any family to speak of. My father died when I was six, and my mom died when I was a baby. My stepmom raised me, but she retired to Arizona about five years ago. We don't really speak much these days."

"No siblings?" Scott asked. "I guess you're a one-of-a-kind, an original." His eyes glittered in the low light of the restaurant.

I decided to ignore the comment as Scott tossed a handful of bills on the table—I noticed that he left a very generous tip—and ushered me out the door. As he deposited me into the car, he snapped his fingers. "I forgot something, be right back, you sit tight." He trotted off back to the restaurant entrance. I pulled out my phone and hit one of my contacts.

"Hi, Mikki! Do you have anything yummy left today?"

Chapter 4

Ten minutes later, Scott and I were seated at a high-top table in the MB Squared Bakery enjoying thick slices of blueberry pound cake slathered in house-made lemon curd.

"I think that I might have to move here permanently," Scott mumbled thickly through a mouthful of cake. "This is absolutely delicious!"

Mikki glided over, a wide smile on her delicate face. "Thank you! Our poundcakes are very popular. We ship them all over the country. The vanilla bean is the most popular flavor, but the blueberry is a close second."

"Do you sell the lemon curd in jars?" Scott asked hopefully.

"Not yet," Michael replied, sliding up next to Mikki and casually draping his arm over her shoulders. "But we've been talking with some folks that could help us get the product manufactured, bottled, and shipped. We'd like to sell our house made jams that we serve with our scones and breads as well." He gave Mikki's shoulder an affectionate squeeze. "Mikki uses a lot of her grandmother's recipes for our condiments, and they've been a huge hit with the customers."

Scott wiped his mouth on a napkin. "I might have some connections, if you're interested," he offered.

Michael reached into his apron pocket and produced a card. "Sounds good, give me a call about it," he said as he handed it to Scott.

Scott accepted and grimaced as his fingers stuck to the card. "I need to wash my hands. I'll be back in a sec." He got up and headed to the back of the bakery where the restroom was located.

Mikki immediately pounced. "Oooh, he's a cutie! And he seems really nice, too!" She gave Michael a friendly elbow to the ribs. "You'd better hope he doesn't move to town, then you might not be the best looking man in Pinewood Corners anymore," she teased.

Michael laughed. "As long as you still think I am, that's all that matters to me."

I felt that weird stab of jealousy in the center of my chest again as Michael leaned over and kissed the top of Mikki's head.

"So do you think you'll go out with him?" she asked me.

"What?" I sputtered. "He's not interested in me, he just wanted someone to show him around town a little."

"Oh, come on. Pinewood Corners isn't that big, he could find his own way around in about an hour. He just said that so he could spend time with you." I tried to wave her off, but she continued. "I'm serious! I saw the way that he was looking at you. He was looking hungrier for you than for the pound cake!"

I shook my head. "I don't believe it, but I sure love to hear it!"

"You just wait and see." Mikki wagged her finger at me.

*   *   *

"It's still a bit early, but I need to get back and let the dogs out for their final run," I told Scott as we pulled out into traffic after leaving the bakery. Scott had purchased half of a pound cake to go—for breakfast, he had said.

"Yes, I need to walk Ranger as well," he replied. "Why don't you leash up your dogs, too, and we can enjoy a walk together." He patted his stomach. "I need to move after all that wonderful food."

I was pleased that he didn't want the evening to end quite yet. We returned to the inn and I noticed that Jared's tan pickup was still parked around the side of the house, next to the detached garage that had once been the stables of the house.

"I wonder why Jared is still here?" I mused aloud as we entered the house. Jared was coming down the main staircase with a flashlight in his hand.

"Power went out," he explained, waving the flashlight. "I had to flip the breakers, but it seems fine now." He gave me a pointed look, but I wasn't sure how to interpret it.

Scott made his way past Jared and headed up the stairs. "I'll meet you right here in five minutes," he said over his shoulder to me.

Jared watched Scott until he disappeared down the upstairs hallway, then turned to me. "Where are you going with him now?"

I bristled at his tone. "How is that any of your business, Jared Baumgarner?"

Jared simply shrugged. "I heard the weeping again, right before the power went out," he told me.

"So are you saying that one thing has to do with the other?" I asked.

"Dunno," Jared replied, "but I wrote it in my notebook."

"Uh, good. Thanks." I waited but Jared just stood on the stairs, so I called to my dogs and gathered their leashes and got everybody ready to go. Scott reappeared just as I was clipping on the final leash.

"Ready?" he asked, opening the door.

It was a lovely fall evening, with a clear sky filled with stars and the air was crisp and invigorating. I felt some of my exhaustion from the day fade away as I took in lungfuls of the cool, clean air.

"You don't get to see stars like this in the city," Scott remarked.

"What city are you from?" I asked him.

"Ranger, stop that!" he cried, pulling up on the dog's leash to stop him from digging at the grass on a random lawn. The dog ignored him and he called out "Ranger!" again.

Weird, the dog doesn't respond very well to his name.

The dog finally stopped pawing at the grass and then squatted. I realized that the dog was a female. *Hadn't Scott referred to the dog as a "he" before?* I honestly couldn't remember.

"Your dog is a girl?" I asked. "I'm sorry, I assumed that Ranger was a boy dog's name."

"What are the names of your dogs?" Scott asked rather defensively.

"Bennie, he's the big brown and white dog, named after one of my favorite songs, 'Bennie and the Jets,' and Henley is the beagle mix, named after Don Henley because I love The Eagles, and the black dog is named Mac, for Fleetwood Mac, of course."

"Of course," Scott replied, "I take it you enjoy classic rock?"

"Yep, it's my favorite type of music." Before I knew it, we were off on a lengthy discussion about classic rock bands and favorite albums. Scott was obviously an aficionado, too, and it was wonderful to talk about a subject I was passionate about with a fellow music lover.

I looked around, suddenly aware that we were quite a few blocks from the inn. "I didn't realize we had gone so far. We'd better start heading back."

"Whatever the lady wishes," Scott said, taking a little bow. I giggled and swatted his arm as we turned around and crossed the street to walk back toward the inn. I felt a flapping around my foot and looked down.

"Hang on, my shoe's untied," I said, bending to fix my laces. Scott paused under a street light, waiting for me. As I straightened, I noticed a poster affixed to the light pole. On it was a photo of a dog with the word "MISSING" in all caps above the dog. According to the poster, the dog's name was

Snowball. The dog in the photo was small, white, and fluffy, and it bore a striking resemblance to Ranger.

"Hey, look," I pointed, "that dog looks just like yours."

"Mmmm," Scott said nonchalantly, glancing at the poster. "It sure does. Poor thing, I hope they find it." He shivered. "Let's get back to the inn, it's getting colder by the minute."

Jared's truck was gone when we returned. Scott and I parted in the upstairs hallway, and I went to my room to get washed up and ready for bed. It wasn't until I was about to drift off into sleep that I realized that Scott had never told me what city he was from.

Spending my nights in the inn brought on new and different dreams. In my dream state, it was as if I was taking the place of the girl I was dreaming about, seeing through her eyes, and her emotions infused my consciousness.

*   *   *

"Please," the voice sobbed inconsolably. "You must listen, before it's too late!"

I strained to hear more, but heard only the sounds of piteous weeping. "Who are you?" I asked, trying to pinpoint where the mournful cries were coming from. "What do you want?"

I strained to hear words within the tearful lament as I felt my way along the wall of the darkened hallway. The feelings of abandonment, utter emptiness, and loss invaded my being and my heart felt as if it were being rendered into pieces, shattering like a vase, like the vase of flowers he had once given me, before he betrayed me …

"You must listen, you must see, before it's too late!"

I crept along in the blackness, terrified and heartbroken. Suddenly, the wall was gone and I was falling, plummeting through empty space, the voice echoing all around me, "Before it's too late, it's too late, it's too late ..."

I sat up with a gasp, blinking in the darkened room. My face felt cold. As I reached up and felt the wetness on my cheeks, I realized that I must have been crying. I wiped at my cheeks and took a shuddering breath to try to calm my pounding heart. Bennie, at the foot of the bed, lifted his head, whined, and thumped his tail on the mattress. I felt more grounded as I rubbed his ears.

"It's okay, boy. I have no idea what I just dreamed, but it must have been a doozy."

*   *   *

The next morning dawned clear and cold. I shivered as I slipped into my robe. Reaching for the door knob, I stopped and remembered that I had a guest. Bennie looked up at me questioningly.

"I guess my leisurely mornings are a thing of the past," I told him. "I'd better get dressed before I go down. It wouldn't do to have the owner lying around in a ratty old bathrobe."

I took a quick shower and put on jeans and a deep purple sweatshirt. I selected a stretchy headband in a lavender shade that coordinated nicely with my shirt. I slicked on a bit of tinted moisturizer and some chapstick and called it a day, since I never wore much makeup. Bennie and the other dogs accompanied me down the stairs, and the cats waited at the bottom.

After everyone had been fed and let out, I noticed the vase of flowers sitting in the middle of the breakfast table. A riot of fall colors—maroon, vivid orange, and deep golden yellow—were accented with gold-sprayed pine cones and brown oak leaves. Next to the bouquet sat a pink box. Atop the box lay a small white envelope.

Inside the envelope was a simple rectangular card covered in neat block letters that read: *"Thank you for a lovely welcome and a great evening. I look forward to enjoying your company again tonight, if you're free. Please enjoy breakfast, on me. I have some business to attend to this morning, but I'll be back later."* The box contained half a dozen assorted donuts. Impressed, I selected a powdered sugar donut and bit into it, showering my chest with a snowfall of sugar.

The front door opened, and Jared's heavy footsteps thumped over the wood planks of the foyer.

"Morning!" he called out as he entered the kitchen. He stopped short when he saw the flowers. "From your guest?" he asked, reaching for the donuts.

"Mmm-hmm," I said through a mouthful of donut. Jared grabbed a maple Long John and half of it disappeared in one bite. He chewed and swallowed.

"I'm going to finish installing the sink in the bathroom of the green room, then I'll get going on the demolition in the cottage," he informed me. "Where's the new guest?"

"Scott," I reminded him, "he said he had some business to take care of this morning, but he'll be back later."

Jared popped the last of the donut into his mouth while I attended to the espresso machine. I handed him a black coffee and he accepted it with a grunt of thanks.

"Festival's kicking off soon," he remarked.

"Yep, I think this year will be the best one yet. Thanks in large part to you, we'll be ready for guests when it starts next week."

"Just doing my job," Jared said. He shifted from foot to foot, sipping his coffee.

"Something on your mind?" I asked him. He hesitated, opening and closing his mouth several times. He took a breath and opened his mouth to speak again, but the sound of the door chimes interrupted him. I brushed my hands together, scattering powdered sugar before I reached for the door knob. Rayna Reese stood on my doorstep, again.

She barreled past me into the lobby, hauling her designer luggage.

"I hear you have a guest, some sort of reporter. I'm check-ing in, too." She strode to the front desk and waited with an imperious air. I rushed around the desk.

"I don't have staff quite yet, they're all starting the day after tomorrow," I told Rayna. "But I can check you in if you don't mind fending for yourself until then, as far as meals and spa treatments, and I'll need you to check out by Monday, when we're officially open for guests, if someone requests your room."

Rayna waved one perfectly manicured hand. "Sure, whatever," she said. "I want your finest room, though."

"I'll put you in the red room. It's the largest room we offer, it has its own fireplace and sitting area, along with an en suite bathroom. No shower, I'm afraid, but the claw foot tub is original to the house and is quite beautiful. I'm sure you'll enjoy it."

Rayna ignored the key I held out and stood looking expectantly at me.

"Uh, right this way," I said, leading her toward the stairs.

"What about my bags?" she asked. I reluctantly grabbed the handles of her suitcases and shouldered her toiletries bag. I reminded myself that this was part of the job as I hauled her heavy luggage up the stairs, wishing fervently that the house had an elevator.

I busied myself behind the desk with the computer. The bookings were coming in fast, and I was thrilled to see that we had filled up for the dates of the upcoming Harvest Happenings festival. I had managed a couple hours of work before Rayna came gliding down the staircase in a cream colored sweater dress with a soft cowl neck and matching cream suede over-the-knee slouch boots. Her ebony hair was piled on top of her head in an elegant updo. She floated into the lobby on a cloud of expensive perfume.

"You look lovely, Rayna," I said, determined to be polite. I was a business owner now, after all. I had to learn to put my personal feelings aside for the sake of the business. I felt sure that I would have to deal with demanding guests every now and then, so I'd best get used to it.

"I'm so relaxed, that tub is amazing, and you've actually provided some nice bath products."

"Glad to hear you're enjoying your stay so far. I only use locally made products, so the bath items are from Elements of Nature, on Main Street. They'll give guests a ten percent discount if you mention that you tried their products here at the Harvest Moon Inn. Don't forget that we've got an indoor hot tub and a sauna in the spa area, and if you'd like, you can schedule the first massage after the spa opens."

"On the house, of course," Rayna said, raising her perfectly arched and shaped brows.

"Of course," I assured her, cursing myself for my inability to stand up for myself. I'd go under in no time if I kept on giving stuff away for free. But I supposed she felt entitled to freebies since, in her mind, she was doing me a favor by staying at my inn and writing it up in her paper. As I was preparing to book Rayna for her massage, the front doors opened and Scott swept in with a sharp breeze and a swirl of leaves.

"Whoa," he remarked as he forced the door shut behind him. "The wind is really kicking up out there." He turned and noticed Rayna.

"Hi," he said, "I'm Scott Carpenter."

"Rayna Reese, editor in chief of the *Pinewood Courier*." She held out an elegant hand. "Enchanté," she said, her voice pitched in a low husky tone that I assumed she meant to be flirty.

Scott shook her hand briefly and dropped it. "Nice to meet you." He turned his attention to me with a warm smile. "Hey, there. You must've had a good night's sleep after our adventures yesterday. You look refreshed and radiant."

Out of the corner of my eye, Rayna pouted. I couldn't help myself, I never got the chance to make a beautiful woman jealous.

"Thanks! And thank you for the flowers, they're beautiful. And the donuts were delicious, that was thoughtful."

Rayna looked as if steam would come out of her ears at any moment.

I gleefully continued, "I managed to clear my calendar this evening, what did you have in mind?"

Before Scott could respond, Rayna interrupted. "I was going to make reservations at Pinewood Steakhouse. If you'd care to join me, Mr. Carpenter, you're certainly more than welcome." She pointedly turned her back to me while making the invitation to Scott.

"No thanks," he said cheerfully and then, to me, he said, "How about dinner and a movie? I hear there's a pretty good pizza place in this town."

"Yes, Marinelli's," I replied. "Its reputation is well deserved, they have great food."

"Six okay for you?" Scott asked me. I agreed and, without another glance at Rayna, Scott bounded up the stairs, presumably to his room.

Rayna huffed. I wondered why she was still standing there with an air of expectation.

Finally, she pointed to the phone on the desk. "Aren't you going to make my dinner reservation for me?" she asked.

"Uh, I guess so. Sure," I said. So Rayna wanted concierge service. Resigned, I sighed and picked up the phone while I googled the number for Pinewood Steakhouse. "What time?" I asked.

After I had secured her reservation, Rayna drifted off to do whatever it was that she occupied her day with. As I worked behind the desk, catching up on emails and phone calls, I saw her sitting on the porch. I had artfully draped some thick flannel lap blankets over the backs of the rocking chairs, and I noticed that Rayna had one wrapped around her shoulders as she sat rocking with a book in her lap. Rayna Reese, whiling away the afternoon reading on my porch. I pinched myself again. It was a miracle that I wasn't black and blue by now, my life was so surreal these days.

After a bit, Rayna wandered back in and informed me that she was going up to change for dinner. I nodded, thinking that her current outfit was far fancier than anything I owned. It occurred to me that I really should go shopping and try to get at least a few decent outfits for business purposes if nothing else. I was intimidated, because I didn't know the first thing about fashion, what was in or out of style, what would be flattering to my figure, such as it was.

I needed help, but I certainly wasn't going to ask Rayna. She would just make me feel like a hopeless blimp. No, I needed someone with more kindness and less extravagant tastes. I typed out a quick text to Mikki, asking her if she had any free time to go on a shopping excursion.

My phone pinged almost immediately with Mikki's reply. *Sorry, Babe, no can do—I'll have to take a rain check. Things are insane at the bakery right now, we're gearing up for increased traffic with the festival and we need all hands on deck. Maybe Lacey could go with you?*

That was an excellent idea, and I decided that I needed to make a run to the library the following day to pick up another batch of my favorite romance novels. I would speak with Lacey about going shopping with me. Even if Lacey's tastes were far more colorful and eclectic than mine, at least she was great company and wouldn't make me feel like a fashion failure.

Chapter 5

The next morning, I was seated in the kitchen, bleary-eyed from my night out with Scott. We had shared a large cheese pizza and garlic knots, and had such a good time conversing about so many subjects that we ended up skipping the movie and moving to Shanahan's Pub to continue talking and ended up in a fiercely competitive game of darts that Scott eventually won. It had been quite late when we returned to the inn.

I was sipping coffee and going through the mail with Bennie and Mac at my feet when Rayna entered the room. She was dressed very casually for her standards, in a pair of trendy designer jeans, low-heeled ankle boots, and a red pullover sweater with a plaid Burberry checked scarf draped around her elegantly long neck.

"Morning, Rayna. Want some coffee?" I held up my cup and gestured toward the machine.

Rayna's mouth stretched open in a huge yawn. "Yes, I would love some coffee." She narrowed her violet eyes. "My sleep was very interrupted last night." She sounded as if she were accusing me of personally conspiring to keep her awake.

"I hope the mattress isn't uncomfortable—" I began.

"The bed is fine, surprisingly wonderful in fact," Rayna interrupted. "The problem is one of the other guests. Their infernal weeping kept me awake half the night!"

I gasped and then tried to cover it up by pretending to cough. "Sorry, wrong pipe," I muttered. "You, uh, you heard someone crying last night?"

"Yes, as I just said, she was very loud. You really must speak with your guests about the noise policy. No one should be making such a ruckus after ten."

"Of course, and I apologize for the disturbance," I hurried to assure her, before she realized that there were no other guests right now besides her and Scott. "What are your plans for today?" I asked, to get her mind off of the subject.

The last thing I needed was for Rayna to get wind of any kind of paranormal activity in my brand new inn and write an article in the *Pinewood Courier* about it. I could just picture the lurid headline: "Are Spirits of the Dead Haunting the Harvest Moon Inn?" While I felt certain that word of the inn being haunted would bring in a certain type of clientele, I wasn't sure that it was the kind of publicity I wanted.

I couldn't explain it, even to myself, but I wasn't ready to share the presence of the weeping lady. I wanted to get to know who she was and what she wanted before I opened the door to the kinds of folks with EMF meters and REM pods and EVP recorders and all manner of alphabet soup electronic gadgets that were supposed to monitor spirit activity. It seemed rude, somehow, to unleash that on this poor soul who was already wracked with grief.

"After I get some coffee," Rayna said, looking pointedly at me and then at the espresso machine, "I was going to run down to the bakery and pick up a danish and then head into the office for a while."

I jumped up and hurried to get Rayna her drink. "How do you take your coffee?" I asked.

"I'll take a caramel macchiato," she replied, "With extra whipped cream." She perched herself on one of the barstools at the island and examined her shiny red fingernails.

"Well, I can offer you anything with milk, regular or oat, steamed or not, and I've got plain old table sugar if you'd like it sweetened."

She sniffed and tossed her long gleaming hair over one shoulder. "Fine, I'll have a latte with regular steamed milk and sugar. You'll need to offer a larger selection of coffee drinks, you know," she scolded. She pulled out her phone and started tapping something on the keypad.

"What are you doing?" I asked.

"Keeping a tab of the positives and negatives of your little inn for my article," Rayna replied.

I swallowed hard and dumped another spoonful of sugar into her coffee.

"Here you go," I slid the mug over to Rayna. She took a sip, then another, and then she started typing into her phone again.

"Where is that charming gentleman, Mr. Carpenter? Has he checked out already?"

"No, he was gone when I got up this morning. I slept later than I intended, after being out quite late." I glanced at Rayna, and I was a little ashamed at how satisfying the look of envy on her face was. I realized my mistake too late. Rayna glanced at me sharply.

"If you were out late, presumably with Mr. Carpenter, then who was the other guest that kept me awake?"

"Actually, you and Mr. Carpenter—Scott—are the only current guests. I'm expecting a lady from a travel website this evening, though."

"Then who did I hear? How secure is this place?"

"It's secure," I quickly assured her. "You probably heard house noises. You know, settling wood creaking and whatnot. Or maybe you heard one of my animals, or Scott's dog, Ranger."

I waited for Rayna's response, holding my breath. I prayed that she was unimaginative enough to buy the explanations I offered. After a moment, she slowly nodded her head.

"You're probably right." She resumed sipping her coffee, and I breathed an internal sigh of relief.

*   *   *

The pungent scent of paper and ink and binding glue wrapped around me like a friendly hug as I pushed my way through the library doors. I inhaled deeply. I had always loved the library. Growing up as a socially awkward only child, books had been my refuge. The characters were my companions through thick and thin, taking me on all their adventures. Amidst laughter, tears, and edge-of-your-seat suspense, books had introduced me to worlds I could never have imagined on my own. They were a welcome escape from a lonely existence.

The library was busy today and was crowded with patrons. The building had recently been expanded and spruced up with a grant from a wealthy patron that the head librarian had become acquainted with and the place was now a modern building with a separate children's library, brand new computer kiosks, a row of private study rooms along the back, and plenty of comfortable seating for patrons and students. There was even a small coffee and juice bar.

My heavy tote bag bumped against my hip as I shuffled toward the book return bin. I fed the books into the return slot and draped the now-empty canvas bag over my arm.

"Hi there, Miss Fancy Inn Owner." A raspy but pleasant voice hailed me from behind the checkout counter. It was Miriam, one of the main volunteers at the library. Miriam smiled, her silver braids swinging as she waved at me.

I grinned back. "Got any new steamy romances for me?" I asked her.

"You bet," she reached under the counter and pulled out a stack of mixed paperback and hardcover books. "I pulled these for our best patron. Four of them are new, and I know you haven't read the Lady Allison series in a while, so I pulled the first three of those for you, as well."

I laughed. "Well, I certainly won't be bored. Thanks, Miriam!'

"I hear you're living your own romance novel lately," she remarked with a wink.

Living in a small town has a lot of perks, but one of the bigger drawbacks is the gossip mill. It was difficult to do anything without having it practically broadcast on a billboard in the center of town.

"I'm sure I don't know what you mean," I stammered, my cheeks flushing.

"I heard he's a real looker, too. Good for you!" Miriam slapped the counter for emphasis. "It's about time you got yourself a man. You deserve to get some—" Before Miriam could complete her moritfying sentence, a spunky redhead dressed in a burnt-orange corduroy skirt with dark brown tights, brown over-the-calf boots and a deep yellow turtleneck appeared.

"Miriam, you're embarrassing the patrons again," Lacey, the head librarian, scolded playfully as she gave me a one-armed hug. "Hi, Colleen, good to see you." She looked me up and down. "I see that romance agrees with you. And I don't mean the books."

"So," I said resignedly, "is everyone in town discussing my love life—or lack thereof?"

Lacey chuckled warmly. "Pretty much. You know how small towns are. Just be happy that it's gossip about something good." She patted my arm reassuringly. "People have seen you out with him at the El, the pizza parlor, the pub." She paused, as if she wanted to go on, but she didn't say anything further.

"I just came in to pick up my fix," I said, pointing to the stack of books on the counter that Miriam was scanning and putting into my bag. "But I'm glad that I caught you. I wanted to know if you would be willing to drive over to Westbrook and go shopping with me this weekend. I'm expecting my first non-media guests on Monday, and I need to spruce up my look a bit."

"Girl, you know I never turn down a chance to shop. Martin's out of town this weekend. He's speaking at an archeological conference," she said, referring to her fiance, who was the youngest son of Sheriff Weaver, "so it's the perfect distraction for me."

"What about Claire?" I asked. Lacey's daughter from her first marriage was four going on fourteen.

"Oh, she's with her father this weekend. Jed and Elaine are going to take her camping before it gets too cold at night."

"Okay then, it's a date! Shall I pick you up?"

"Perfect. How about Saturday at 10:00?"

We agreed on our plan, and I left the library with a full bookbag and a light heart. The afternoon was crisp and the sky was a brilliant topaz blue dotted with pure white cotton ball clouds. The breeze whipped the dried leaves along the sidewalks, frustrating the merchants attempting to sweep the walkways and set up their harvest displays.

I hummed softly to myself as I strolled along Main Street, taking in the fragrance of autumn. The Java Hut smelled wonderfully earthy and rich from the scent of freshly ground coffee beans. The bath and body store, Elements of Nature, had their doors propped open and the scented oil diffuser just inside the door pumped out a spiced, woodsy vanilla aroma reminiscent of the crisp leaves skittering past my feet.

The town had hung up cheerful banners with colorful autumn leaves and pumpkins around the borders, proclaiming the Harvest Happenings festival dates. The Main Street merchants had hung up fliers advertising the town's most popular dance of the year, the Harvest Moon Masquerade Ball. It was a formal event, but guests were encouraged to wear masks with their suits and ball gowns. I loved it because it was in the spirit of a regency romance novel.

Even though I always went single, I never missed it. I had only one "gown" that was actually an inexpensive Regency Halloween costume that I had bought years ago at one of those Halloween specialty stores that pop up in empty storefronts every August and September. It wasn't that fancy, but it did the trick.

I realized that I could afford to upgrade to a better gown if I wanted to this year and made up my mind to keep an eye out when Lacey and I went shopping on Saturday. I continued on until I came to Deann's Donuts. I saw a sign in the window proclaiming "Yes, We Have Cider Donuts!" and made a beeline for the shop.

"Hi, Deann!" I called as the bell over the door tinkled merrily. "How's it going?" The scent of frying oil and yeast and sugar surrounded me.

Behind the counter, a stout woman with short and curly brown hair partially covered by a paper wedge cap smiled, showing the gap between her front teeth. "Hey, Colleen, gorgeous day today. I hear the inn is shaping up nicely."

"It definitely is," I replied, agreeing to both of her remarks. "Can I please get two of your cider donuts?"

"Coming right up." Deann snapped open a small white paper bag and reached her gloved hand into the case and pulled out two donuts. As she handed me the bag, she added, "Also heard you're seeing somebody."

"I guess you can't keep any secrets around here. We're spending some time together. I don't know how much longer he's in town, though. He's a freelance writer."

"I heard he's easy on the eyes, but a bit of a scoundrel."

I cocked my head to the side, puzzled. "Scoundrel? What do you mean?"

"Darlene told me that he stiffed her on the tip the other night," she replied, wiping down the already spotless gleaming white counter.

"But I saw him leave a generous cash tip," I protested.

Deann shrugged. "If it was cash, maybe someone else took it before Darlene could pick it up," she said.

I grabbed onto the excuse like a lifeline. "Yes, that's probably it," I said. "Maybe some kid, grabbing money for a new Xbox or something." I held out a five dollar bill. "Thanks for the donuts, keep the change."

I wandered back onto the sidewalk and sank down on a nearby bench, lost in thought. I watched the people walking around, out and about doing business or running errands. For the first time since I was six, I felt like part of the community instead of a pariah. I was finally getting some attention from an attractive man that I had so many things in common with, I had a small circle of friends, and I had found a place in the local merchant's community.

For the first time in my life, I felt a sense of belonging. I had lived here all my life, but I had always felt like an outsider, looking in. Now that I had finally made my way toward the inner circle, I was afraid of slipping back into outcast status.

Removing a warm donut from the bag, I bit in and chewed. The tart sweetness of the apple and warm cinnamon sugar exploded in my mouth. The outside of the pastry was perfectly crunchy and sugared, while the interior was tender and moist. My eyes rolled back in my head with pleasure. The food did the trick, as usual. The sweet and comforting donut made me feel infinitely better. I was reaching for the second donut when someone sat down on the other end of the bench.

"Hiya. Is that one of Deann's cider donuts?" Jared raised his eyebrows until they disappeared under the bangs of his bowl haircut. I held the bag out to him. I told myself that I certainly didn't need another donut.

Jared practically snatched the bag out of my hand. "Thanks. I came into town to run to Crawford's Hardware. The inn is ready to go, so I'm going to focus on the cottage. I figure that I'll be able to get it gutted and the plumbing and electrical updated before we need to discuss paint colors and interior and exterior finishes and whatnot." He paused to take a huge bite of donut.

While he was chewing, I took the opportunity to ask, "Do you think the construction will disturb the guests?" Before he could answer, I snapped my fingers. "Oh, that reminds me, Rayna heard our weeping lady last night!"

Jared choked on a bite of donut. I whacked him on the back. "Do you need something to drink?" I asked, anxiously peering at his purple face. He shook his head, still gasping.

"I'm okay," he wheezed, leaning forward with his hands on his knees. "What do you mean she heard the weeping lady?"

"Exactly what I said. She was all bent out of shape this morning, complaining that she couldn't sleep because of the noise. I tried to get her off the track because I don't need her painting the inn as some sort of spook central in her little article." I leaned back on the bench and closed my eyes. "I want people to feel like they can come to my inn with their pets and relax in peace, and not have to worry about being kept awake by restless spirits."

I felt a warm hand pat my knee. "Don't worry about it. I might be worried if it was anyone else, but knowing Rayna, she'll find something to distract her soon enough."

When I opened my eyes, the hand was gone. Maybe I had imagined it.

I sighed. "I sure hope so. She'll be checking out tomorrow, anyway. And that woman from the travel blog should be here this afternoon." I checked my phone. "I need to run, I want to get back to the inn and put some fresh flowers in the guest room before she arrives." I rose from the bench.

Jared pitched the wadded up paper bag into the nearby trash can. He thanked me for the donut and ambled off down the sidewalk.

I was driving back toward the inn, and I navigated past the Fresh Stop, the main grocery store in Pinewood Corners. I turned into the parking lot, intending to buy some flowers. I hated to admit it, but Rayna was right. I would need to offer more coffee drinks, and Michael from the bakery had shared his tips on preparing several types of drinks with my fancy espresso machine.

I wandered down the aisle where the coffee and trimmings were. I selected several roast levels of whole bean coffees as well as a decaf version and multiple flavors of syrups. I stopped along the back aisle to pick up extra milk and some canned whipped cream, along with a couple tubes of pre-made cinnamon roll dough. I wasn't the best baker when it came to yeast dough, but at least I could pop these in the oven and the kitchen would smell delicious. I grabbed a cheerful autumn bouquet from the floral display near the checkout. At the last minute, I backtracked to the drugstore section and, after a moment of hesitation, dropped an additional item into my cart.

When I returned to the inn, everything was quiet. I greeted my pets, and let the dogs out for a bathroom break, including Ranger, whom I had to let out of Scott's room. I hoped he didn't mind, but I didn't think it was fair to keep the poor dog cooped up all day.

I trimmed and arranged the flowers in a quaint pitcher that was part of an antique wash stand from the room where the new guest would be staying. For a moment, I was overwhelmed by the strong and powdery scent of lilacs, which was odd, since there were no lilacs in the bouquet or anywhere nearby. Shaking it off, I stood back and admired the overall effect. The flowers looked absolutely charming poking out of the unusual container. Satisfied, I carried the pitcher toward the staircase.

I was halfway up when I walked right through an icy cold spot, like a passing through a freezing waterfall. I shivered violently, almost dropping the pitcher. I paused, stepping back for a second. It wasn't my imagination. There was definitely an area, about three feet in circumference, that was markedly colder than the surrounding air.

I started to shake with an overwhelming feeling of terror and dread. I nearly fell to my knees. I squeezed my eyes shut and breathed deeply, concentrating on the feel of the stairs under my feet and the pitcher clutched in my hands until the emotions passed. *How weird.* I would have to ask Jared to check the ventilation system and make sure there wasn't anything wrong with the furnace.

After I had placed the pitcher in the room—the perfect finishing touch—I went back downstairs to find that Scott had returned from wherever he had been. He was standing in the kitchen, frowning down at Ranger.

"Why is my dog in the kitchen? I left her shut in my room this morning," he addressed me as I entered the room.

"Hello to you, too. I decided to let her out for a run with my dogs when I returned from running some errands today. I hope that's okay, I just thought she had been shut in for a while, and she'd appreciate some fresh air. Not to mention that I didn't want her to, uh, mess up the floors."

Scott looked chastised. "You're right, of course. I'm sorry, dear, I do trust you. I didn't mean to overreact. It's just that I have some sensitive paperwork in my room, proprietary materials for some things I'm working on. I wouldn't want anyone else having access to snoop around, you understand. And hello." He smiled and my heart melted at his expression, not to mention the endearment he had dropped so casually.

"I didn't go into the room, I promise, I just opened the door and let the dog out," I reassured him. I leaned back against the edge of the large kitchen island.

"Good," Scott said. He came over to stand in front of me, his hands resting on the counter on either side of where I was leaning. He was close enough that I was breathing in the woodsy notes of his cologne and I could feel the warmth radiating off his body. "What are your plans tonight?" he asked me, smiling seductively. His breath was minty, fresh and cool, yet warm as it brushed over me.

My blood hammered in my ears, thudding so loudly with the beating of my heart that I thought I might go deaf or pass out, or maybe both. "Um, I went to the library today. I was just going to curl up with a good book." My voice cracked at the final word, and I cleared my throat.

"Mmm, you smell really nice," Scott leaned even closer, inhaling. "What are you wearing?"

"It's soap," I blurted out, feeling dizzy as the room wobbled at the edges of my vision.

"Well, it's a lovely soap. Your hair looks really cute today, too. I like that headband." His fingers reached up to touch the circle of fabric.

"Thanks, I have it in lots of colors. I'm trying to grow my hair out, you see. I've had it short for absolutely years and years, and I thought, you know, that it was time for a change, so I'm growing it out some. It's rough going at first, though, because it's just at a weird in-between length and I can't really do much with it, so I got a bunch of headbands and that helps to keep it out of the way until it's long enough to—" I stopped short when I realized that Scott's face was inches from mine, his finely chiseled lips parting for a kiss.

Chapter 6

"Whoo, the traffic is getting busy out there!" Rayna trooped into the kitchen, her boots clicking on the tile floor. Scott quickly pushed himself off the edge of the island in one smooth motion and turned to Rayna.

"Ah, yes, I've seen all the banners, posters, and fliers about the festival around town." He gestured to me. "I was just about to ask the lovely Colleen here if she'll escort me to the ball."

I was floored, to put it mildly. I stood there blinking and gaping like a fish. My heart was still hammering from the near-kiss, and now Scott was asking me to the ball. I glanced around for a paper bag in case I started to hyperventilate. Rayna did a double take.

"So what do you say?" Scott asked, cocking one eyebrow in my direction, hands on his lean hips.

"You're staying in town that long?" I asked, stalling for time because I wasn't sure he was serious.

"Sure, why not? I'm happy to relocate to another hotel if you've got guests coming and need my room. I want to write a rather extensive piece, not just on your inn, but on the town and the festival. I think it will do well as a regional flavor article," Scott explained. "I would love to attend the ball. It seems like a pretty big deal around here, and I can't think of anyone I would rather have on my arm than you." He beamed at me.

Rayna frowned. "What publication did you say you work for, again?" she asked.

"I didn't, I'm a freelancer," Scott told her as he plucked an apple from the bowl on the island. "Why don't you and I discuss the ball over dinner?" he suggested to me before he bit into the apple with a loud crunch.

Unable to speak, I nodded mutely as he strolled out of the kitchen.

Rayna's intense gaze lasered in on me. "What is all that about? Why is he taking *you* to the ball?"

I was still stunned by Scott's words, but I wasn't that far gone. I stiffened. "Excuse me, I'm not exactly whale chum, you know. I'm a single woman, he's a single man. Why shouldn't we spend time together?"

"Yes, but he's so … and you're like …" she gestured at me, waving her hands up and down.

"Just say whatever it is you're trying to say," I spat through my teeth.

"I mean that he's so hot, and you're overweight and plain, your face isn't even that pretty. You have a choppy haircut, and you dress like a farmhand. The only thing you have going for you is money, but I have that, too. It makes no sense whatsoever," Rayna crossed her arms over her chest, as if daring me to contradict her.

I was shaking with rage. I was sick and tired of everyone treating me like a doormat, ignoring me or insulting me. I felt my body fill with indignation like water into a vessel, and my vision turned white at the edges and I began speaking, but the words felt like a foreign language in my mouth.

"Rayna, that's a terrible, rude, and mean thing to say. I want you to apologize to me right now or get out of my establishment."

"Oh, please," Rayna flapped her hand at me. She looked unconcerned that her words might be painful. Was she really so clueless? Or just massively self-centered?

"I'm one hundred percent serious. Apologize or leave." I pointed to the door. "You need to come down off your high horse, Rayna, and realize that there are other people in this world besides you!"

Rayna sucked in a breath. "Fine," she huffed. Turning on her heel, she stomped out of the room. "But don't think I'm going to write anything nice about this wretched establishment," she called over her shoulder.

Trembling, I sank onto one of the barstools at the island. I felt both hot and cold sensations like wild rivers rushing through my body. Now that my eruption was over, the rage that had filled me slowly drained away. I heard a door slam hard from upstairs. Hot tears stung the corners of my eyes as I drew in a shaky breath and slowly released it.

Digging my fingers into the edges of the stool, I fought the strong impulse to go after her and apologize, and beg her to stay. I was woozy from my outburst. I had never stood up for myself like that before, I had no idea what had come over me.

The thought of Rayna being upset with me was eating me alive. People pleasing was an extremely hard habit to break. I rode it out, letting the anxious feeling roll though me as I tried to reason with myself. What could Rayna really do? Nobody took her articles very seriously, and it wasn't like the *Pinewood Courier* had the distribution of a paper like the *New York Times*. Even if she trashed my inn in print, it would only be a minor blip. But still, it wasn't like me to behave like that. I had almost felt as if my personality had been temporarily overshadowed and the words that had flown out of my mouth had come from someone else.

I ran my hands over my face and tried to get myself together. I was filling the kettle at the sink when I heard the sound of heavy footsteps and luggage rolling over the wood flooring of the lobby, followed by the slam of the front door. I took a deep breath and let it out slowly. At least the altercation had gone down before the new guest arrived. I had to be pleasant and welcoming when she did, so I chose a chamomile and mint tea bag to both calm me down and lift me up.

The bell on the front desk rang out just as I took the first sip. Cursing under my breath as I scalded my lip, I set the cup down with a snap and hurried to the front. The bell had been Jared's idea. He thought it would lend an air of old fashioned charm to the inn, and he was right. I put on a big smile and entered the lobby.

"Hello, and welcome to the Harvest Moon Inn. I'm Colleen Perkins, the proprietor." I greeted the casually dressed woman waiting at the desk. She was an older woman, tall and lean with wiry gray hair worn in a short and spiky cut, deeply tanned leathery skin, and a wide smile that showed a row of gleaming teeth. Her red-framed glasses were so large they covered half her face. Her pale green eyes twinkled as she greeted me.

"Hi, there. Pat Jennings, from *Travel Well*," she extended one thin brown hand. I liked her immediately. She had a very friendly and down to earth vibe. I got her checked in and led her to the green room.

She glanced around. "Nice. I like that wash stand, it's very authentic. Nice touch with the flowers, too."

"Thank you, I hope you have a pleasant stay. You can reach me by dialing the extension listed by the phone. Please don't hesitate to let me know if you need anything at all. There are brochures in the lobby with local restaurants and activities if you're interested. And feel free to use the hot tub or sauna if you'd like."

I left Pat to unpack and get settled in and returned to the kitchen to resume my cup of tea. As I brought the cup to my lips, Scott entered the room.

"Where would you like to go for dinner this evening?" he asked me, crossing to the refrigerator and pulling out a Sprite. He cracked it open and took a sip, sighing with satisfaction. "I love Sprite, it's my favorite soda."

I set the cup back down. "Mine too!" I smiled affectionately at him. "We've had dinner at the El, and we had pizza last night. You're spoiling me, you know."

Scott sat down across from me. "I like spoiling you. You deserve to be spoiled."

I felt my cheeks flush and quickly said, "How about some Mexican food? There's a great place on Oak, it's called Casa de Alimento."

"The house of food?" His left eyebrow shot up.

"How do you do that?" I demanded.

Scott lifted one shoulder. "I don't know, it's something I've always been able to do. But I can only raise the left one. If I try it with the right eyebrow, I just look like someone squirted hot sauce in my eye."

I laughed as the intercom on the kitchen wall buzzed. I went to answer it, and it was Pat as I had expected, since she was the only other guest at the moment. She wanted to know which of the restaurants was the most fun, and I recommended the El for an entertaining atmosphere and great fried pickles.

"Jared is so smart, he hooked up this system so that we can talk to the guests from almost anywhere in the house," I remarked as I returned to the table.

"I thought he was finished here," Scott sounded cranky.

"He's working on the cottage in the back of the property where I'll eventually be living," I said, confused at Scott's sudden turn of mood. "It used to be the groundskeeper's cottage."

"Well, he doesn't need to come into the inn, then," he sulked.

"What's wrong?"

"Nothing, I just don't like the way he acts so familiar around you," Scott replied.

I was stunned. He was actually jealous. Of Jared Baumgartner. "You think that Jared—*Jared*, of all people, is romantically interested in me?" I scoffed. "Let me assure you, we've known one another for years and he's like a cousin or brother to me. We're just comfortable around each other *because* we're so familiar."

This weird jealousy thing was a new situation to navigate for me. Many of the romance novels I read presented a jealous suitor as evidence of passion, but I tended to agree with the stories that showed jealous behavior as more of a red flag that a person might have a tendency toward a controlling nature.

Looking somewhat mollified, Scott picked up the can of soda and took a long drink.

"Okay, if you say so," he muttered when he finally came up for air.

"I know so." Deciding to give Scott the benefit of the doubt, I rose to go to the sink and pour out my now ice-cold cup of tea. "What time do you want to go to dinner?"

*   *   *

The hostess gave Scott a wide smile as she pulled menus from the side of the podium.

"Table for two? Right this way." Hips rolling, she led us through the maze of tables to a booth along one wall. As I dragged myself across the vinyl seat in an ungainly scooting motion, the hostess handed Scott his menu, brushing her fingers across his. Shooting me a hostile look, she tossed my menu down on the table in front of me and sashayed away. I had never realized the mental fortitude it took to be out and about with a person who was so much more beautiful than you are.

I picked up the menu and studied it. Distracted by the feeling of eyes on me, I glanced over to see Scott sitting with his elbows on the table, chin in his hands, staring at me, his chiseled lips turned up at the corners in a bemused expression.

"What?" I asked, running one hand over my head self-consciously. "Is my hair sticking up? Do I have something on my face? I hate it when that happens, even to someone else, because then you have that internal dilemma of 'should I say something?' because I may embarrass them. But what if they get mad at me for not saying anything when they discover later on that they have chocolate smeared around their mouth? But I know that when I have something on my face or in my teeth or something, I sure hope somebody says something to me, because—"

Scott's finger brushed over my lips like a feather, making me shudder. His hand then caressed my cheek, which felt like a hundred needles of fire dancing over my skin. "Shhh," he whispered. "Nothing's wrong. I just like looking at you, that's all." He smiled.

My gaze was glued to the tabletop. I couldn't look up, for fear that I was hallucinating the whole thing. There was no way a man this gorgeous was into *me*. I squeezed my eyes shut, mentally counted to three, pinched my thigh under the table, and opened them. Scott was still there, across the table. He grasped my hand in his.

"I can't wait to show you off at that ball, if you'll have me as your escort," he said, giving my hand a firm squeeze and releasing it as the server approached with bowls of salsa and a basket of warm tortilla chips, still shiny with oil from the fryer and glistening with salt crystals.

I ordered a Sprite, of course, and the cheese enchilada combination platter, with beans and rice. Scott chose a black bean tostada and a chile relleno, a la carte, and a Sprite.

"So," he remarked, settling back to wait for the food, "tell me about yourself. How did you come to purchase the inn?"

"Well, I came into some inheritance unexpectedly, and I was working as an assistant manager at the Pet Palace in town. I just love animals, as you know." I took a sip of my soda and cleared my throat. "I just wanted to open an inn that catered to pet lovers, because my favorite part of my old job was meeting the customers and their pets, and I had always loved the McIntyre house, so it seemed like a natural fit."

"Mmm," Scott murmured as he reached for a chip and dunked it in the extra-spicy salsa. I followed suit, selecting the mild version to dip into. The salsa was cold and fresh, bursting with the acidic sweetness of tomatoes and pungent onion and cilantro that complemented the crisp saltiness of the warm tortilla chip perfectly. Sheer heaven.

"You do have some management experience, then." Scott observed, sipping his soda. "Do you have any hospitality experience?"

"I took a pretty thorough online course on hotel operations and management," I replied somewhat defensively.

Scott picked up on my tone immediately. "I wasn't implying that you were unfit to run the place," he said, holding up his hands. "I just meant that you seem to be a natural."

I laughed. "Sure, ask Rayna about my wonderful customer service skills."

"Don't worry about her, I'm all too familiar with her type. Rich, spoiled, no respect for anyone who doesn't belong to daddy's country club." His voice had taken on a hard edge and his eyes became blue flames as he bitterly continued. "She'll never know what it's like to struggle, and someone like her will never understand what it's like to come from nothing and have to battle for every scrap."

He opened his fisted hand, and the chip he had been grasping was crumbled nearly to dust. He cleared his throat noisily and wiped his hand on a napkin. Before I could speak, he said, "Sorry about that, her kind just triggers me." He took a deep breath and let it out slowly. "But I want to hear more about you, I want to know everything." His cerulean eyes now sparkled. The haunted and angry look was gone so quickly that I wondered if I had imagined it.

"Well, there isn't much of interest. I was born here in Pinewood Corners, but my mom died when I was just a baby. My father remarried when I was four, to my stepmom, Peggy. My dad and I had a special bond, I really loved him. He was my hero, my everything. He called me his 'little pumpkin.' It was just the two of us until Peggy came along, and I guess she made my dad really happy."

I looked back down at the tabletop and absently took a chip from the basket and began snapping off pieces of it, dropping them onto the little plate in front of me. "But my dad died when I was six. Car accident. Peggy raised me, but she didn't really like me all that much."

Scott started in his seat, reaching for me, but I waved him off.

"Oh, I don't mean that she was abusive or anything, but she just signed on to marry my dad, and be a stepmom, not to be a single mother. She was …" I searched for an appropriate word, "adequate, I guess. She kept a roof over our heads and kept me clothed and fed and everything. And she never remarried. But she was never really a role model for me, and we didn't have a close bond. Nobody expected my dad to leave us so soon, especially not Peggy."

"I'll bet she cut ties as soon as her obligation was done, right?" Scott asked, his tender gaze softening the harsh truth of his words.

"Pretty much. She lives in Arizona now, in one of those planned adult communities, and she loves it. Bridge club, golfing, aqua aerobics class, bingo, line dancing at the community center, and all that sort of stuff. She keeps herself pretty busy. We do the obligatory birthday and Christmas calls."

Scott reached across the table and took my right hand in both of his. "I'm sorry you went through that."

I tipped my head in acknowledgment of his sympathies, too shy to respond. I had a reputation for talking too much, but I wasn't used to being so vulnerable with my words.

"I visited the historical society museum today," Scott announced. I was grateful for the change in subject to something less emotional.

"Oh? What did you think about the history of our little town?"

"Very interesting," his gaze intensified. "I spent quite a while viewing the necklace."

I knew he was referring to the famous 15 carat heart-shaped ruby necklace set in platinum with diamond accents. The necklace had been a town legend, connected to the previously missing wife of Merrick McKinney, the founder of Pinewood Corners.

Through diligent research and determination, Martin Weaver, son of the town sheriff, and Lacey Crawford, the head librarian, had solved the mystery of the missing wife and located the lost necklace. In the course of their research, they had also discovered that the founding family hadn't quite died out as previously thought. It turned out that I was actually the last living descendant of the founding family, and no one had been more stunned to learn that fact than me.

"Really?" I asked. "What did you think?

"It's gorgeous," Scott replied, reaching for me again, "just like you."

I pulled my hands away. "Scott, you really have to stop that." My voice came out harsher than I had intended.

"Stop what?" he leaned back, frowning.

"Telling me that I'm gorgeous and lovely and things like that. I'm about as lovely as—as a—as a basket of chips. I know

I'm not beautiful. I've never even really had a romantic relationship before," I finished, my voice dying to a whisper.

Scott leaned forward. "Listen to me, and look at me." He
tipped my chin up with his fingertips. "Look at me, Colleen,"
he repeated and waited until I reluctantly met his blazing blue
eyes with my own before he continued. "You may not see it,
but I do. You are the kindest, most generous, loving, graceful
and humble soul I've ever met. Your beauty runs deep, and I
see it. I see *you*, Colleen, and you *are* beautiful."

My mouth opened and closed, trying and failing to form
a response.

The server chose that tender moment to approach with
our entrees.

"Here we go, folks. Plates are hot!" She plunked the thick
white oblong plates down in front of us, and we assured her
that we didn't need anything further at the moment.

I was beyond grateful for the distraction. Scott's speech
had floored me in more ways than one. I had never heard
words like that, other than in my romance novels or maybe
dialogue from a movie. But to hear them in real life, directed
at me, was totally surreal. I fought the urge to pinch myself
again. We both dug into our meals with gusto and by the time
we came up for air, the emotional tension had dissipated.

"That necklace must look fantastic on you," Scott
remarked, popping the last of his chile relleno into his mouth.

"I have never actually *worn* it," I cried. "I've never really
even thought about taking it out. It's safe in the museum, with
the best security case and alarm we could get, and there's a

security guard on duty 24 hours a day. I'm more of a jeans and sweatshirt kind of gal than a diamonds and rubies type, anyway."

Scott dabbed his mouth with his napkin. "Well, I understand that this ball coming up is pretty formal. I'll have to rent a tux, I suppose. But what I really want is to show you off, like I said. And you're beautiful, like I also said. I want everyone to see what I see. They just know you as 'good old predictable Colleen.' I want to show them glamorous and gorgeous Colleen. If you're wearing that necklace, I guarantee that you'll shine like the sun."

I blushed. "Oh well, I guess I would probably be allowed to wear it, if I really wanted to."

"Allowed?" Scott sounded appalled. "It belongs to you, nobody has to give you permission. Just tell them you want to wear it. They can't stop you. It's entirely up to you, but I'm telling you, you'll be the envy of every woman in town."

I promised that I would think about it. Truthfully, the idea of wearing something that was worth so much money, and yet at the same time priceless, made me sweat with anxiety. What if I damaged it somehow—or heaven forbid—lost it? I shuddered. It was insured, of course, but I would be heartbroken if it was gone, lost to history once again. On the other hand, envisioning myself being the envy of every woman in town was a new sensation and just thinking about the confidence boost that being seen in the famous necklace would give me was enticing. It might even bring good publicity for the inn.

We agreed to split an order of flan for dessert. The creamy custard coated in luscious bittersweet caramel soothed my mouth and stomach after the spicy meal.

The server deposited a small black folder on the table. "Whenever you're ready, no rush," she assured us as she hurried away.

Scott reached into his jacket pocket. With a look of concern growing on his face, he began patting his jacket and pants pockets.

"What's wrong?" I asked.

"My wallet," he replied, "I swear I put it in my jacket before we left, but it's not there. I can't find it anywhere."

I reached for my purse on the seat beside me. "That's okay, I've got it." Scott started to protest. "I insist. Consider it a payment for listening to my boring life story."

"Colleen, you shouldn't insult yourself so freely. Some people will take you at your word."

Chapter 7

Saturday morning found me up extremely early, thanks to the intrusive dreams that kept me from sleeping well the night before. I sat yawning over my coffee, trying to make sense of it all. I was rather ashamed to admit that I had taken to sleeping with the ear plugs that I had picked up at the Fresh Stop the other day to block any sounds that might keep me awake, including random unexplained weeping. But earplugs couldn't stop me from dreaming.

The dreams had been vague, with a wild mix of sensations ranging from love, longing, and adoration to sorrow and terror. I had vague impressions of the face of an older, angry man with a flowing mustache, long skirts swirling, a set of shimmering golden eyes and a set of snapping black ones, a trunk tumbling end over end down a set of stairs, its lid popping open and spewing clothing in all directions, and the terrifyingly jarring sensation of falling that had woken me before dawn.

Glancing at the clock, I figured that I should probably eat something before I had to get ready for my shopping date with

Lacey. The sun would be up soon. I rose from the barstool, shooed Lemon down from the countertop, and shuffled to the fridge. The cat shot me an indignant look and stalked away, striped tail twitching.

I spotted the packages of cinnamon rolls that I had purchased earlier and felt a surge of happiness. After fiddling with my fancy new oven, I finally figured out how to preheat it to the temperature specified on the label. The cardboard tube gave a satisfying pop when I whacked it on the counter top, releasing the spiral segments of dough. I placed the rolls on a baking sheet and popped it into the oven, setting the timer and heading to the espresso machine to make another coffee.

As I waited for the machine to brew my shot of liquid energy, I glanced out the window. There was a light bobbing around the cottage. Someone was on my property. Without stopping to think, I grabbed my cell phone from the counter and a heavy-duty flashlight from one of the drawers and slipped out the back door.

The chill of the early morning air penetrated my thin sweatshirt, and I shivered as I crept to the cottage, dialing the sheriff's office to report an intruder as I went. I hung up once the dispatcher, Mindy, assured me that a deputy was on the way. She had also ordered me to return to the safety of the main house and wait for the deputy. I promptly ignored her advice and continued toward the cottage, emboldened by the substantial weight of the flashlight gripped in my hand.

"Whoever you are, you are trespassing. I've called the sheriff, they're on the way," I called out in the gruffest voice I could muster. I got no response. I felt as I had when I had become enraged at Rayna's insults, fed up and ticked off and spoiling for a fight.

I marched up the sagging steps of the small porch and stomped to the front door. I flung it open, prepared for battle, and shone the flashlight's beam directly into the face of Jared Baumgartner. He stumbled back, eyes bulging and mouth wide open in surprise. His face was so comical, I couldn't help myself and I started laughing hysterically. When Jared stumbled backward and landed on his butt, I howled.

"What's so funny?" he asked irritably.

I wiped my eyes and tried to catch my breath. "Oh, Jared, you just looked so startled, and then you fell on your—" I was interrupted by Deputy Tom Willis running across the yard, shouting, gun drawn. I turned and waved my hands in the air. "Hi, Deputy, it's all right, false alarm. It's only Jared."

The deputy came bounding up the steps, his tall form making the porch seem even smaller. The radio on his shoulder crackled. Mindy's voice came through, asking whether the deputy needed backup. Deputy Willis assured her that the situation was under control before he holstered his weapon and addressed me.

"Morning, Colleen. I'm glad everything's okay, but why did you think Jared was an intruder?"

"I saw a light moving around out here, and it's so early on Saturday morning, and I thought … Jared, why are you here on a Saturday?" I turned to address the bewildered handyman.

Jared was back on his feet, wearing a pair of dingy gray coveralls spattered with various colors of paint. His brown eyes seemed half vacant. "I dunno, I couldn't sleep and I kept thinking about this place and all the projects that need to be done, and I just felt like I needed to get over here and get to work right away. It's like I had to come as quick as I could because the place needs me. I haven't hooked up the generator yet and I was using a flashlight." He blinked and seemed to come back into himself as he turned to me. "I'm sorry, I should have told you that I was here, but I thought you'd still be asleep for a few more hours and I didn't want to disturb you or the guests."

"I was up, I couldn't sleep, either. I was just making some breakfast—" I gasped and shrieked, "My rolls!" as I took off running full tilt back to the house, leaving the two men gaping after me.

I burst through the backdoor to find utter chaos. The oven timer was frantically beeping while the smoke alarm on the wall blared in reaction to the black clouds pouring out of the oven. Waving the smoke away from my face, I slapped the button to turn the oven timer off as I grabbed a thick kitchen towel and pulled the tray out of the oven.

Coughing from the burnt-smelling fog. I carried the tray outside and left the door open to air out the room. The rolls were sad blackened lumps huddled on the tray. I glanced up at the house. All the windows were still dark. Thank heaven for small favors and old, thick walls.

I heard wild laughter from behind me, and I knew that Jared was enjoying his admittedly rightful retribution for me laughing at him earlier. I looked over in his direction where he stood with Deputy Willis. They were both doubled over and roaring. I smiled ruefully.

"Don't worry, the new cook, Mrs. Blake, starts on Monday," I told them.

*   *   *

Half an hour later, the deputy had departed and I was seated with Jared at the kitchen island enjoying a freshly brewed cup of coffee and the second package of cinnamon rolls. Jared had insisted on making this batch, and he teased me mercilessly about my cooking skills as he did so.

I was reaching for a third roll when Scott strolled into the room. He was wearing a dark blue button up shirt under a soft pale gray pullover sweater with charcoal gray slacks that showed off his slim yet muscular form. His wavy black hair was slicked back with what looked like some sort of gel, and he looked good enough to eat.

"Morning," he greeted us as he headed straight for the espresso machine. After he had his caffeine fix in hand, he returned to the island and pulled out the stool next to mine. He smelled wonderful, sweet and musky with a hint of leather.

"You're looking lovely this morning," he commented to me. He looked around and sniffed at the air. "What's that smell? Did something burn?"

I felt a blush creep from my hairline to my collarbone. "You could say that," I admitted.

"Don't worry, I saved the day and made another batch," Jared shoved the plate of iced rolls in Scott's direction. With a grunt of acknowledgment to Jared, Scott took one of the pastries.

"What are your plans today?" Scott addressed me, but Jared answered him.

"I'm hoping to finish up the strip out and removal of the debris in the cottage today, so I can get started on the structural work first thing next week. I need to prepare the landscaping for winter, too. That patch of primroses around the oak tree is still huge, even this late in the year. I've never seen anything like it."

Annoyance flickered across Scott's face. "That's nice. I was asking Colleen about her plans for the day." Jared ignored Scott's irritated tone and placidly kept on munching.

"I'm going shopping with my friend Lacey in Westbrook. I'm picking her up at ten," I said.

"That sounds like a fun trip, too bad a mere male can't join." Scott grinned.

"Oh, did you want to come? I didn't think—"

"I'm just teasing you, darling. I have plans to meet with Michael Brandon from the bakery this morning to discuss that contact I mentioned, the one that can help him with his product manufacturing and distribution. And I need to do some work on my article this afternoon." He shot me a dazzling smile. "I've been too lax with my work lately. There are too many charming distractions in this town." He looked directly at me, his strong brows and the corners of his full lips raised. I looked down at the tabletop, which seemed to be my usual move these days.

I was relieved but didn't want to show it. I thought of Lacey's reaction to me showing up with Scott in tow and shuddered. A man on a shopping trip with two women usually entailed said man sitting in chairs outside various dressing rooms, holding shopping bags and trying to look patient. I was so grateful that I didn't acknowledge Jared shooting a dark look at Scott when he had so casually called me "darling."

*　　　*　　　*

At 10:00 sharp, I pulled up in front of a small house that was painted in cream with red trim. The lawn was browning with the advent of fall, and the trees were dropping leaves across the yard in shades of brown, yellow, and orange. The front door opened and Lacey came bouncing out dressed in a pair of bright red jeans, a pink sweater with white stripes under a red and white coat, and chunky white sneakers. She plopped onto the passenger seat and promptly took control of the music. I pulled back into traffic to Stevie Nicks warbling out "Bella Donna."

Lacey leaned back, her copper curls fanning out over the headrest. "I am SO ready for a girls day out," she sighed. "I need a break from all the wedding planning. I think I'm about to give up and elope."

"What does Martin say to that?" I asked.

"Oh, he says I would regret it later on. He's probably right, but don't tell him I said so." She pulled her ringing phone out of her large red leather tote bag and swiped the green button and listened. "Claire, honey, if your daddy says it's safe, then it's safe. There is no such thing as bigfoot, I promise. Now you be a good girl and have fun. I'll see you tomorrow night. Love you, Claire-bear." She hung up and chuckled. "Poor thing, she stumbled across one of those shows about bigfoot hunters, and now she's scared to go camping." She dropped the phone back into the depths of her bag.

"I don't blame her, those shows can be pretty frightening." I shuddered.

"Anyway, what's new with Mr. Hottie?" Lacey rubbed her hands together gleefully in anticipation of some juicy gossip.

"There's not much new to tell. Oh, he did ask me to go to the Harvest Moon Ball with him."

Lacey's deafening shriek caused me to jerk the wheel and I momentarily veered into the next lane, earning a honk and an angry gesture from the driver currently occupying that lane. I corrected our course and Lacey apologized.

"Sorry if I overreacted. I'm just so happy for you, and I *knew* that he was romantically attracted to you." She began humming the wedding march tune.

"Yeah, yeah, so you say. You just focus on your own wedding, and I'll try to get us to Westbrook in one piece."

Lacey dug around in her tote and pulled out a bag of trail mix. She waved the bag at me. "Want some? No? Hey, we should stop by that formal wear place in the mall and look at ball gowns!"

"Do you need to buy a dress for the ball?" I asked her.

"I'm wearing the gown I bought the year before last. My budget this year is going toward my wedding dress. I offered to wear my dress from my first wedding, to save money, but my Aunt Denise insists that it's bad luck." She rolled her eyes. "We need to find something stunning for you. You can't keep wearing that old Halloween knockoff when you'll be on the arm of Mr. Moviestar Handsome."

I laughed and resigned myself to the fact that Lacey was determined to make this out to be the romance of the century. I still wasn't so sure, but it was a lot of fun to pretend.

*   *   *

I squinted into the row of full-length mirrors at all five images of myself. "I guess I do like the satin trim and bow in the back on this one," I admitted, turning to look over my shoulder. I had tried on at least a dozen dresses already, and Lacey kept coming in with piles more draped over her arms. None of them had seemed right. The dressing room curtains parted and she came in again, triumphantly holding up a padded satin hanger bearing a black gown with a full skirt and embroidered red roses.

"Try this one," she said, thrusting the pile of black lace and tulle at me.

After some struggle, I was fastened into the gown and turned to look in the mirrors. I was surprised at my reflection.

I never would have chosen an off-the-shoulder style with three-quarter sleeves in sheer black wrapped with roses that hit just below my elbows, but I felt like a vision in this dress.

Embroidered blood-red roses and leafy emerald vines decorated the neckline and sleeves, flowing over the bodice of the dress and dripping tendrils down the folds of the full skirt. The way the floor length gown gathered in the middle and then flared out made my waistline look smaller, minimized the size of my hips, and gave me the appearance of an hourglass figure.

I was worried that the black would wash out my pale complexion, but the roses helped reflect a becoming glow to my cheeks, and the fringe of off-the-shoulder black lace hit low enough that the expanse of my skin looked creamy and lush in contrast. The black was edgy and the roses were traditionally feminine. It was a perfect balance. The gown was romantic and gothic and ideal for an October ball.

I sighed and turned in front of the mirror, scarcely believing that the lovely, feminine creature staring back at me was really the same woman that had walked into the store in faded jeans and a baggy gray sweatshirt. Lacey slipped through the curtain and stopped short. She let out a long, low whistle of admiration and dropped the pile of dresses she was carrying.

"Whoo, girl," she flapped her hand in front of her face, fanning herself. "You look *hot*! Like, 'get me a glass of ice water and a fan' hot!" She stepped over the pile of glittering sequins and lace on the floor and reached for my hair, sliding off the pink and white headband. "We could get you hair extensions and do a nice, elegant updo, and I could help you with your makeup, and we'll find the perfect supportive undergarment, maybe a nice long-line bra, and you'll need some jewelry to complement this gorgeous neckline."

She gathered the top of my hair and piled it on the crown of my head as best she could, demonstrating as she spoke. My mind went straight to the ruby necklace. *The necklace would look stunning with this gown.*

I glanced at the price tag and almost fainted. I had paid less for my first car. Granted, it had been an old clunker, but still. "This dress is too pricey," I exclaimed, immediately struggling to extract myself from it.

"Relax, it's on sale," Lacey assured me, pointing to the sign advertising a store-wide 40% off sale that was running. The store was smart to run the sale during the run up to the ball.

"I guess that makes it a little easier to swallow the price," I admitted, "but it's still a lot of money."

Sensing the hesitation in my voice, Lacey put her hands on my shoulders and met my eyes in the mirror. "Listen, you look absolutely amazing in this gown. You've tried on dozens and didn't get a hit. I saw the way you were looking at yourself in this one. You saw yourself as a beautiful woman, the beautiful woman that you already are. She came out of hiding in this dress, and you deserve to be that woman every day."

Her words called up Scott's previous ones, when he had also insisted that I was beautiful. Maybe he was being sincere.

Maybe there really was a glimmer of beauty somewhere within the plain and plump girl who talked too much.

"I'll take it," I said, blinking back tears.

*   *   *

Several hours later, we were heading back toward Pinewood Corners with a trunk filled with shopping bags and shoe boxes, and the ball gown hung on a hook over the back passenger seat, encased in a shimmering pearlescent plastic zippered garment bag bearing the name of the boutique in purple cursive letters.

"I'm exhausted," Lacey announced, taking a long drink from a straw that ended in a loud and rude slurping sound as she polished off the iced coffee that she had bought on our way out of the mall. She burped gently.

"I'm so glad that Claire is with Jed this weekend," she continued. "I'm going to take a nice long candlelight bubble bath and read that new fantasy romance that I brought home from the library yesterday. A hot forbidden entanglement between a gorgeous Elven princess and a Fae warrior sounds like just the thing I need to chill out tonight."

"That does sound pretty good," I agreed. "Pass it on to me when you're done?"

"Sure thing," she grinned at me. "Need some passionate inspiration, eh?" She winked playfully as I shook my head and laughed at her one-track mind. I decided to change the subject.

"So is the harvest moon actually in October?" I asked my well-read and educated friend.

"No, the full moon in September, which is closest to the autumn equinox, is actually the traditional harvest moon," she replied.

"Then why do you think the town calls the ball in October the 'Harvest Moon Masquerade?'"

Lacey lifted her shoulders in a brief shrug. "I suppose the town council feels that it sounds better than the 'Blood Moon Masquerade,' although I think that sounds marvelous." Her green eyes sparkled with mischief. "But I'll admit that it totally changes the vibe of the event. Instead of the elegance of *Emma*, the theme would be more akin to *Pride and Prejudice and Zombies*."

I laughed at the thought. "Why is the October full moon called the Blood Moon?" I asked, genuinely curious.

"Traditionally, October was the month that folks did their hunting to put up meat for the winter, so a fair number of animals were killed," she replied.

I shuddered. "Have I mentioned how glad I am that I was born in modern times?"

"So were they," Lacey replied. "Every person is living in their own modern times."

"How do you consistently boggle my mind?"

Lacey tipped an imaginary hat. "Just one of my many talents, ma'am."

I dropped Lacey off in front of her house and left her to her bath and book. I headed to the inn, my mind wandering down paths of possibility that I had never before allowed myself to entertain.

I imagined the coming days and months filled with romantic and mundane dinners with Scott, deep conversations, attending the Lights by the Lake holiday festival together, going ice skating and attending the tree lighting on the town square—and in the spring, picnics by the lake.

I even allowed myself the luxury of imagining myself standing by Scott's side in the gazebo in the park, wearing a white satin gown and sheer veil while a string quartet played Pachelbel's "Canon in D" and friends all around …

The car vibrated violently, the wheel shaking in my hands like a living creature, and I realized that I had drifted far enough to the right that my tires were hitting the curb. Shaking myself mentally, I gripped the steering wheel tightly and pulled back into the center of the lane and forced myself to focus on the road.

I scolded myself for putting the cart before the horse. In reality, I barely knew Scott. I had no idea where he came from, and I knew nothing about his family or background. I resolved that the next time we were alone together, I would take the time to ask Scott to share more about himself.

I wanted to enjoy the process of taking things slow and getting to know him. The idea warmed me from the inside out and, feeling immensely better, I switched the radio on and hummed along with The Eagles' "Take It Easy" the rest of the way home.

Chapter 8

I pulled into the driveway that ran along the side of the inn and parked my SUV near the kitchen door. As I opened the back hatch, Jared shuffled around the corner of the building. His coveralls were gone, and he was dressed in his usual jeans, work boots, and flannel shirt.

"Looks like you had a successful shopping trip," he remarked as he came to stand beside me and peered into the back of the vehicle. Without asking, he reached in and started gathering up bags and boxes into his arms and carried them toward the house. "Want these up in your room?" he asked over his shoulder.

"Yes, please," I said, then added a hasty "and thank you!" before Jared disappeared through the door. I grabbed the few bags that were left, along with the gown that was hanging in the back seat. As I entered the kitchen, I spotted the new guest, Pat Jennings, sitting at the kitchen table with a pot of tea, her grayed head bent over an open laptop.

"Hi, there," she greeted me enthusiastically as I kicked the door shut behind me. She rose and crossed the room in a few quick strides. "Let me help you with that," she said, lifting the satin hanger from my hand. She pulled the zipper down a few inches and peeked into the garment bag. "Sorry, I can't help myself—I'm unrepentantly nosy," she informed me. "This is an absolutely gorgeous gown! For that ball that I've seen advertised all over town?"

"Thanks, yes," I replied, setting the rest of my bags down on the island. "I went on a shopping excursion today."

"You did well, if that man that just came through bearing piles of merchandise was any indication."

"Oh, that was the handyman, Jared. I did find a lot of great stuff. It was a fun day. Fun, but tiring," I said. The sunlight slanted through the windows and I realized that it was getting on toward late afternoon. "I'm sorry that we don't have our cook yet," I started to say, but Pat cut me off.

"Oh, don't worry about that. This place is delightful, and this town is so much fun. I absolutely loved the El Royale diner. Darlene, the owner, and I really hit it off. She invited me to her weekly poker game tonight!"

Uh-oh, I thought. Darlene was notorious for being as shrewd a card player as Doc Holliday himself. I hoped Pat knew what she was getting into.

"Don't you worry," Pat assured me, as if she had read my mind, "I'm a seasoned player."

"Seasoned player at what?" Scott asked as he entered the room. My heartbeat quickened at the sight of him.

"Poker," Pat explained. "I play all kinds, Texas hold 'em, 7-card stud, draw, Chinese—you name it, I can play it. I'm not too bad at bridge, either, and if there's a bingo game in town, you'll usually find me there. I love games of chance. Strictly low-stakes, you understand. I'm not looking to lose my life savings or anything."

"Really?" Scott's eyebrows rose. "How do you feel about investing? It's the ultimate game of chance."

"What did you have in mind?" Pat asked, clearly intrigued. She peered at Scott over her snappy red frames.

Scott pulled out a business card. "Let's get together and discuss it before you leave town. I dabble in some investment strategies."

Pat accepted the card and studied it briefly before sticking it in the pocket of her royal blue cardigan. "A travel writer *and* an investment guru, eh? A real renaissance man."

Scott's stormy blue eyes narrowed. "What do you mean by that?" His voice took on an almost hostile tone.

Pat wasn't phased at his shift in mood and she calmly replied, "Nothing at all, just observing your multiple talents." She closed the laptop and carried the teapot and mug she had used to the sink. "I need to run along and change. I'll just leave you two young folks to enjoy your evening. Don't wait up!" She gave a cheerful wave on her way upstairs.

Jared came clumping into the room just as Pat exited. "I put everything on your bed, I hope that's okay." He noticed the packages on the island and pointed to them. "You want me to take those up, too?"

"Um, sure, if you don't mind," I told him, observing that Scott's stormy look was back. "And you should probably go ahead and take off after that. You've worked hard all day."

"Yes, Jared, you really should go now," Scott said, moving closer to my side. "Colleen and I will be leaving shortly. I've made reservations at the Pinewood Steakhouse for the two of us this evening."

"What?" I stepped away from Scott. "I'm sorry, but I don't remember firmly agreeing on plans for dinner tonight."

Scott's blue eyes turned the color of a stormy sea, and I hurried to explain.

"I mean, I appreciate you making reservations and all, and Pinewood Steakhouse is really a lovely place, they actually have quite a few great vegetarian options, I really love their pasta primavera, it's delicious. But I'm just really tired from shopping all day and I was planning to just make a sandwich or something and relax with a book tonight, maybe turn in early. We walked around a lot today, and I think I didn't drink enough water. I might be a little dehydrated, and I just need to relax and freshen up. I'm sorry." I gulped. I was monologuing again.

I could tell that Scott was upset. His jaw muscles worked as he drew in a deep breath. He finally let it out in a long sigh.

"No, I'm the one who should be sorry. It was overstepping to assume that you would be free and wished to go out with me tonight. I should have asked you first." He nodded briefly as he headed for the door. "Excuse me, I need to cancel those reservations."

The guilt trip descended right on cue. Now I felt bad that I had disappointed Scott, and possibly even embarrassed or emasculated him. The familiar drumbeat of self flagellation began. *Why do I feel so awful? I have a right to say no, a right to spend my evening however I feel is best for me. Why am I so consumed with anxiety about Scott being upset with me? Why am I cursed to be such a people pleaser?*

I was so lost in my morose thoughts that I jumped when Jared spoke.

"Hey, it's okay. He's a grownup. He'll get over it." I felt a large hand rest a moment on my shoulder.

"Thanks, Jared," I said, trying to keep the looming tears from thickening my voice. I was grateful that I had my back to him so that he couldn't see how raw and vulnerable his kindness made me feel.

"Night," he replied. I listened to his boots thumping across the floorboards as he left.

*   *   *

Just as the feisty chambermaid was about to lock lips with the handsome rogue of a sea captain, a barrage of knocking assaulted my ears. I jumped as I dropped the book and it bounced off the edge of the mattress and onto the floor. I clutched my chest, patting my rapidly beating heart.

"Yes?" I called, trying to sound as if I hadn't just about come out of my own skin.

"It's me, Scott," the voice on the other side of the door was quiet and unsure. I sat up and swung my feet to the floor.

"Come in," I called, patting down my rumpled hair and tightening the sash on my new flannel bathrobe that matched the pajama set I wore underneath.

The knob turned and the hinges squeaked as the door drifted open. Scott stood there clutching the handles of a large paper bag. "Since you were too tired to go out, I brought dinner to you." He held the bag up as an offering, his face contrite. "I apologize if I sounded upset earlier. I admit that I was very disappointed because I had been looking forward to spending more time with you."

I softened at his conciliatory tone, and at the smell coming off the bag he was holding.

"It's okay, I understand," I said. "What have you got in there?" I raised my chin to indicate the takeout bag.

Scott held up one finger. "First things first, I want you to climb back into your bed and get comfortable. Then, you get your surprise."

"Oh, thanks, but you don't have to serve me, I can come down and eat in the kitchen, it's fine. I'll just grab my slippers and you can—" Scott shushed me with a finger to my lips.

"Hush now, you deserve a little spoiling once in a while. You've had a long and tiring day. Get back in that bed right now!" He playfully pointed to the bed with a devilish smirk.

As I settled in, Scott popped briefly back into the hallway and returned bearing a lap tray that he positioned over me in the bed. He then reached into the bag and produced a square styrofoam box that he placed on the tray. When I reached for it, he gently swatted my hands away. "Patience," he admonished playfully.

He proceeded to pull out a china plate that I recognized from one of my hutches downstairs, and a linen napkin rolled around cutlery. He removed the contents of the styrofoam container onto the china plate. I started laughing at the image of the pile of good old macaroni and cheese gracing the delicate china. Scott paused.

"What's wrong? Don't you like macaroni and cheese?" He looked unsure, his eyes wide and anxious.

"Oh, no, I love it," I assured him. "I've just never had it on a fancy plate like this before." Scott's features relaxed into a wide smile.

"Then you'll also love this," he said, pulling out a second, smaller but no less elegant plate, onto which he placed a slab of chocolate cake. He finished off the setup by pouring a can of Sprite into a gorgeous cut-crystal goblet. The clear sparkling soda reflected the fiery opalescent shimmers in the crystal patterns of the glass. Scott stepped back with a bow.

"Your dinner is served, m'lady." He started for the door. "Let me know when you're done, and I'll come and take the tray."

I frowned. "You're not staying?"

"I've already had dinner," he explained.

"Well, then, you can just keep me company while I eat," I indicated the chair off to the side of the room.

"If you're sure you aren't too tired," Scott began.

"No, please, I would love to talk with you," I insisted.

Leaving the door wide open like a perfect gentleman, Scott lowered his masculine frame into the delicately framed needlepoint chair. He grimaced. "I feel like I'm going to break this thing," he commented.

"Don't be silly," I said. "You're in better shape than I am, and I haven't broken it yet. I did break a chair once, but that was a long time ago, and the chair was really old, probably dried out wood and bad hardware, so it was no surprise. Anyone would have collapsed in that thing—even a child could have broken it, so sometimes it's not the person but the chair."

Silently, I admonished myself. Scott was right. I had to stop being my own worst critic and putting myself down to other people all the time. And I had to get a grip on my nervous rambling. Even though I certainly was nervous, considering the handsome man sitting a few feet from me in my bedroom, even if the door was open and everything was above-board. This particular scenario had certainly never happened to me before.

I inhaled deeply and let my breath out slowly. I picked up the fork and began eating. The macaroni had the perfect al dente bite and the velvety cheese sauce was salty and intense with extra sharp cheddar umami flavor, and the pasta was still warm. I knew it was from the El because I had enjoyed this dish many times before. It was one of my all-time favorites.

Scott perched on the chair, looking expectantly at me as I ate.

"What did you want to talk about?" he asked.

"You," I replied. "Where are you from? Tell me about your family. I want to know all about you." I put my fork down and focused on Scott.

He shifted uncomfortably in the chair. "I don't really like to talk about my family. I lost my parents and brother in a house fire years ago. I wasn't in the house. I was staying the night at a friend's house. I … I wasn't there to save them." He stared at the floor the entire time he spoke, blinking rapidly. I could barely hear him whisper, "It was the worst day of my life."

"That must be painful to carry," I said softly. The only sound in the room for the next few moments was the gentle ticking of the second hand of the clock on the wall.

"Well, anyway, how's the meal?" he asked briskly, finally looking up at me.

"Oh, it's delicious, thank you. How did you know it was one of my favorite dishes at the El?" I picked up the fork and resumed eating.

His eyes sparkled with mischief. "I may have asked the waitress if she knew what your favorite was."

"Oh, you may have, eh?" I scooped up another forkful of noodles, held them up in salute, and popped them into my mouth. Given Scott's obvious discomfort with speaking about his family, I allowed the subject to drop.

We ended up discussing the various types of macaroni and cheese dishes, including stovetop versus baked, and the merits of add-ins such as bacon, jalapeno, or chili—with and without beans. We also split the piece of cake, but shared a fork, which was surprisingly intimate to me.

After I finished eating, Scott took the tray and dishes and departed with a chaste kiss to my forehead, closing the door behind him. As I lay on my pillow, drifting into sleep, I regretted that once again, Scott had not revealed much about himself and his background other than that he had lost his family. It must have been very painful for him, judging by his emotional reaction. I was determined to know more, but I would have to tread lightly.

*   *   *

I was terrified of the snapping black eyes and booming voice. I backed away, putting distance between us, clutching the wall.

"How could you?" the man with the black eyes roared, waving the small red leather-bound book at me. "We're ruined!" He flung the book at me. Dried petals flew out from between the pages and fluttered around me as I ducked and stumbled back, my feet tangling in my long skirts, and I felt myself falling backwards.

I tried desperately to grab at anything as the fingers of gravity wrapped around my shoulders and pulled greedily at me. The black eyes widened. His hands reached out, clutching at thin air as I flew back. His voice screamed my name as I fell, feeling my own scream building in my throat as my body plummeted downwards ...

The screaming and pounding went on and on and on. I sat up in bed with a gasp and realized that the pounding was coming from my door.

"Colleen? What's going on? Are you all right?" The voice on the other side of the door belonged to Pat Jennings, and she sounded very concerned. "Colleen, I'm going to call the police!"

"No, it's fine, I'm okay," I called, fighting to disentangle myself from the damp sheets that were twisted around my body like an affectionate snake. I finally freed myself with shaking hands and stumbled toward the door and flung it open.

Pat stood in the hallway, phone in hand. She was fully dressed and not in pajamas.

"What time is it?" I asked.

"It's two thirty in the morning," Pat replied. "I just got back from my poker game, and I heard this awful screaming coming from your room. You sounded like you were in serious trouble, but the door was locked."

I scrubbed my face with my hands and blinked in the light blazing from the sconces along the hallway. "I was having an awful nightmare. I was definitely in serious trouble because a super scary man was very angry with me. He was yelling at me for something that he said 'ruined' him. It was terrifying, and then, in the dream, I fell down the stairs." A shudder wracked my body, and I wrapped my arms around my torso tightly, trying to stave off the chills.

Pat pulled me into the hall by my elbow. "Let's go downstairs and I'll make you a pot of tea—caffeine-free, of course—and you can tell me all about your dream. You're not going to be able to get back to sleep any time soon, anyway, and I'm pretty good at dream interpretation."

"Dream interpretation?" I asked, my mind still fuzzy from sleep as I followed numbly behind Pat. I hesitated at the top of the staircase, the dream of falling still very fresh in my mind. I told myself not to be silly, it was only a dream, and I certainly couldn't continue to live in a two-story house where I was afraid of the stairs. Sucking in a deep breath, I put one foot in front of the other and forced myself to descend the stairs, although I clung to the banister with a white-knuckled grip.

Pat led me to the kitchen and settled me at the table while she bustled around, filling the electric kettle with water and dropping several Sleepytime tea bags into one of the ceramic teapots that I kept in a glass-fronted cabinet.

"So, in this dream, were you watching it as if watching characters on a television screen, or was it first person, as if you were looking out from the eyes of one of the dream characters? And were you yourself in the dream, or do you feel that you were someone else?" Pat set the teapot and two mismatched mugs on the table. She pushed the pink cup with the gold trim toward me and kept the white mug that declared "Morning Person" in green letters and an upward pointing arrow for herself.

"Are you a morning person?" I asked her.

"Sure, if you count the fact that I'm usually awake into the wee hours of the morning, I'm absolutely a morning person." She poured the steaming tea, delicately minty and pale yellow, into my mug. "Now, please answer my question about your dream."

"It's over now, I'm fine. I appreciate your concern, and thanks for the tea, but I don't see how discussing it is going to help."

Pat sat the teapot down on the trivet with more force than necessary. "Colleen, I heard you thrashing around and shouting in your sleep last night, too. Something is going on here. I can hear a lady weeping on the staircase, and there is a distinct cold spot on the landing. I can smell ladies' perfume, lilac to be exact, in odd places as well, and you don't wear perfume, I don't wear perfume, and I doubt that the handyman or Mr. Carpenter are slathering themselves in lilac-scented eau de toilette."

"We have bath products in the rooms and the spa," I offered, but Pat shook her head, her long silver filigree earrings swaying.

"That was the first thing that I thought of, but none of the products in my room contain any ingredient remotely like lilac." She raised the mug to her lips, blowing across the surface before taking a small sip. She set the mug down and sighed deeply. "Colleen, I have a confession to make. I came here under false pretenses."

I blinked at her in confusion. "But your name is real, at least your ID matches the name you gave me."

"No, not a false identity. I really am Pat Jennings, and I really do write for a blog called TravelWell. What I didn't disclose was that I came here because I was interested in the history of the house, and all the rumors about it being haunted or cursed." She settled in, elbows on the table, and continued her story.

"My twin sister, Natalie, and I used to be a paranormal team. Both of us had mediumship abilities and a knack for helping spirits move on to the other side. We cleared some miserable and mischievous spirits and helped them move on from a lot of places and helped a lot of terrified people get their homes and lives back. The travel blog came later, after my sister passed away. I didn't want to continue the paranormal business without her. I couldn't exactly be a part of Pat and Nat without Nat, could I?" She smiled, a faraway look in her eyes.

"I'm so sorry you lost your twin sister," I said.

"Oh, it's all right," Pat assured me calmly, "She's still in touch with me all the time."

I rubbed my eyes, half convinced that I was still asleep. Surely I had heard incorrectly. I looked at Pat calmly sipping her tea.

"What are you talking about?" I finally asked.

Pat tapped the side of her head and chuckled. "Psychic medium, remember?"

I smiled and blushed. "Of course," I replied, even though I didn't understand much about the paranormal or what mediumship entailed. When I said as much to Pat, she tried to give me a quick rundown.

"Most of the time, a person passes and their spirit moves on immediately from this plane, and they're gone. However, sometimes a spirit has unfinished business or feels a need to warn loved ones of danger, like they need to stay on to guard a place. Sometimes they go so suddenly, they don't even realize that they're dead. There are many reasons a spirit may choose to stay on this plane. But ultimately they don't belong here, and they usually end up doing more harm than good and eventually become frightening entities that terrify the living."

She paused for a drink of tea before continuing. "That's where my sister and I would come in. Natalie was very gifted.

She could actually dialogue with spirits. I mostly get impressions, visions, and feelings. That's harder, because I have to try and make sense of the feelings or visions and interpret them, and it's easy to go wrong when you don't know the person because they died a hundred years ago."

She held up her hand. "Now, don't get me wrong, I have no intention of writing up some lurid piece of horror about this place. I just saw the photo of the front of the inn and I just knew something was off here. I thought I could just check in for a few days, and if there was a paranormal issue, then I would see if my help was welcome. If not, then I would still have a pleasant stay in a charming town and write up a mundane article about it. No harm, no foul, I had nothing to lose. So here I am, and there's definite paranormal activity." She stopped speaking for a moment and looked gravely at me. "So is my help welcome?"

I hesitated to answer. I had guests coming in two days. This was all too much, and it was way too late in the night. What Pat was telling me was too incredible to be believed, and yet … I thought of how I felt my father's presence sometimes, and the cold spot on the staircase, the weeping lady that both Jared and I had heard, the mysterious figure in the upstairs window, the heart-stopping terror I felt in the vivid nightmares I was having every night since I moved into the house, the scent of lilac perfume in the air where it didn't belong, and I knew deep down that Pat was right. Something far beyond the ordinary was definitely going on in my dream house.

Chapter 9

"Morning!" Pat slid onto the barstool next to me at the kitchen island. She was wearing a pair of dark-washed jeans and a long flannel red and black buffalo plaid duster over a black top and she sported a set of long jet beads around her neck.

"How do you look so chipper?" I asked through a yawn. "We were up talking half the night."

Pat smiled as she selected an English Breakfast tea bag from the assortment in the basket on the counter and dropped it into a sturdy white ceramic mug. "I'm just lucky, I guess. I've never needed much sleep. And I'm very glad that you're open to investigating further. I'm going to start with the historical society. It's closed today, but the gentleman who runs it, a guy named Martin Weaver, has agreed to meet me there." She glanced at the slim newspaper that sat near my left elbow. "Is that today's paper?"

My mouth twisted into a wry grin. "You are very generous. This little thing is the latest weekly edition of the *Pinewood*

Courier. We don't generate enough news to warrant a daily paper." I handed the paper to Pat. "You're welcome to it. It's mostly ads for local merchants and information about the current festival activities. And Martin Weaver is sharp as a tack. He's engaged to marry one of my best friends. He also teaches history at the local high school."

Pat accepted the paper and the donut I offered her—store bought, of course—and took her breakfast out onto the front porch. I sighed and put my head down on my arms and closed my eyes. I was almost asleep when I felt a feather-light touch brush the back of my neck. My eyes fluttered open and my heart leaped. *It must be Scott.*

I lifted my head and turned to greet him. To my surprise, Jared stood behind me. He was dressed much more formally than usual in a pair of pressed navy chinos and a blue and white striped button up shirt. His dark brown loafers looked freshly polished, and his bowl cut looked like it had been brushed vigorously, and the static caused the edges of his fine light brown hair to float around his head.

"I hope I'm not too early, but I wanted to get here before the employees arrive." He shuffled his feet awkwardly.

"Not at all. I'm glad you're here. I was up half the night, and I don't think there's enough coffee in the world to help me feel ready to face the new employees on my own." I held out the plate of donuts and Jared selected a maple bar, as I had known he would. "You look very nice, by the way," I added.

Jared's neck turned bright red, and the redness crept all the way up until it disappeared under his hairline. His jaw worked as he rapidly chewed and swallowed.

"Thanks," he brushed at the shower of crumbs on his chest. "I wanted to look a little more professional than when I wear my coveralls." He polished off the remaining half of the donut in a single bite and washed it down with a swig from the coffee he had brought with him.

"Why were you up half the night?"

"Because I had an awful, violent, and frightening dream. Apparently I was screaming so loudly that Pat thought I was being attacked. She was pounding on the door, about to call the police, when I woke up. We came downstairs and talked for a while." My eyes widened as it occurred to me that Jared had been having experiences with the house as well. "Jared, you should talk to her, too. She knows a lot about this kind of stuff."

Jared dug around in his pants pocket and produced his little notebook. He opened the cover and flipped through to a blank page, took the little pen from the elastic loop on the side, and began scribbling.

"What are you writing?" I leaned forward, straining to see.

"I'm recording your encounter," he explained without looking up.

"It wasn't an 'encounter,' it was a dream."

Jared didn't reply. He just kept on scratching the pen across the pages. After a few moments, he snapped the cover shut and replaced the notebook in his pocket.

"I'm writing it down; it could be important," Jared said. His brown eyes darted around the room. "Is Carpenter around?"

"I haven't seen Scott yet this morning, why?" I felt defensive at his tone when he said "Carpenter."

Jared looked hesitant, glancing around and shifting from one foot to the other. Finally, he pulled out a barstool and perched on the edge of it. He leaned toward me and spoke in a low whisper. "I've been working on the cottage the past couple of days, and I've felt and seen some odd things. I need to show you—"

"Good morning," Scott sauntered into the kitchen, freshly showered, his black hair still damp. His jeans were faded in all the right spots and wrapped around his lean hips like a glove. I was practically salivating. Scott paused on his way to the espresso machine, observing Jared leaning in close to me. "Am I interrupting something?" he asked tersely.

"You're not interrupting, not at all," I assured him.

"What is *he*," he pointed a finger at Jared, "doing here so early? What exactly does he do for you?"

"Jared handled the renovations, and he was kind enough to be on hand to welcome the new employees."

Jared's eyes narrowed and he leaned back, crossing his arms over his chest.

I held up the plate. "Donut?"

Scott shook his head and resumed making his coffee. "No, thank you. I've had too much good food in this town, I need to cut back." He patted his perfectly flat stomach.

Jared rolled his eyes, and I kicked his shin.

"Ow!" he cried.

Scott shot a sharp look in our direction.

Desperate for a new topic, I asked, "How did you sleep?"

"Like a rock. I've been up for a while. I took Ranger out for a run and then hit the shower. I'm heading out to interview Mayor Reese this morning for my article."

He leaned back against the counter and sipped his coffee. The golden morning sunlight flooding through the window behind him lit him up with the glow of one of DaVinci's angels, highlighting his high cheekbones and sharp jawline.

"What have you got on the agenda today?" Scott asked.

The doorbell chimed. "I'm doing orientation with my new employees, and it sounds like they're starting to arrive, if you'll excuse me," I replied, hoisting myself from the barstool. Jared dutifully followed as I made my way to the front door.

Betsy Killian stood on the porch, her fine pale hair pulled up into a flimsy fluff of a ponytail on the side of her head. I spotted others pulling up in cars or coming up the walk. Spa therapist George Hall was gallantly escorting my cook, the widow Rowena Blake, up the walk as his wife, Lisa, trailed behind them. Mrs. Blake looked tickled pink to be on the arm of the handsome and muscular George, who bore an uncanny resemblance to Chris Hemsworth, the Australian actor. Amy and Lori, the two college girls that I hired for the front desk, were getting out of a little red Toyota, and Sandy Wilcox, the new housekeeper, was coming up the walk behind Lisa Hall.

Eugenia Higgins, my other housekeeper, had been hired some time ago and knew the ropes already.

I welcomed everyone into the east parlor where we had tea, coffee, and donuts and got to know each other. We toured the house and the spa and pet salon. I gave everyone a rundown of the expectations of their respective positions, and Jared was extremely helpful answering questions about the building and the renovations, as well as the intercom system details.

Mrs. Blake loved the kitchen and we discussed her ideas for various meals that she could prepare and leave in the freezer and refrigerator for me to be able to heat and serve when she was off duty, which thrilled me. I had no desire to repeat the incident with the cinnamon rolls.

I had set up an account at the Fresh Stop for Mrs. Blake to purchase groceries for the inn, and had set up something similar with Elements of Nature for the spa products that Lisa and George would be using. I wanted to keep things as local as possible to help support my fellow merchants.

As I escorted my new team to the front door, I felt like I had hit the jackpot. Everyone seemed to get along well. The girls, as I had already begun to think of Lori and Amy, were already good friends, and Mrs. Blake loved teasing George about his looks and light-heartedly ganging up on him with his wife, Lisa. Sandy and Betsy were becoming fast friends, and I noticed that they were walking out together, talking and laughing.

I closed the door and leaned against it with a sigh.

"That went well, don't you think?" I asked Jared.

"They seem like a good group," he replied.

"Thanks, by the way. For recommending them, and for being here today. I couldn't have answered all those questions about the renovations."

Jared cleared his throat noisily and his ears turned red. "It's almost lunch time. I was wondering, if you're hungry, maybe—"

"Scott, you're here! I didn't realize you were back from your interview," I cried as I spotted Scott at the top of the stairs.

"I wanted to get back here in time to take you out to lunch. I keep hearing about this sandwich place called Logan's."

"Yep, that's a great spot for lunch. Their roasted veggie sub is amazing. They use a balsamic glaze that's to die for."

As Scott descended the stairs, my gaze was glued on his fine form. George may have been more of a beefcake, but I only had eyes for Scott's tall and lean figure.

Scott finally reached the bottom of the staircase and held out his elbow. "Shall we?"

Laughing, I put my hand into the crook of his arm and replied, "We shall!"

I was so enthralled that I didn't notice Jared follow us onto the porch and down to Scott's car. I did notice when he started to get into the back seat.

"Jared, what are you doing?" I was genuinely puzzled.

"I thought we were going to lunch," he replied placidly.

"You're not invited," Scott's voice was cold and blunt. "Get out of my car."

I gasped and my face must have reflected how horrified I felt, because Scott added a reluctant "please."

Jared's eyes met mine in the rearview mirror. He mouthed the word "later" and exited the car.

Soon Scott was holding the door open at Logan's Lunch, and the divine scent of fresh baked bread wafted out. I inhaled deeply.

"Mmm, is there a better smell on earth than fresh bread?"

Scott mumbled a reply that sounded a lot like "money" but when I asked him to repeat it, he brushed it off.

We approached the counter, where the owner, Kyle Logan, was taking orders. I introduced Scott, and Kyle smiled broadly.

"Oh, Scott here has come in several times this week," he pointed at the menu board on the wall behind him, "You want the usual three-meat with bacon?"

My mouth dropped open and my eyes popped. Scott hurriedly corrected Kyle.

"I'm a strict vegetarian, you must have confused me with another customer."

Kyle leveled his gaze on Scott, looking skeptical. "I guess so," he finally said with a shrug. "Anyway, what will you have today?"

I ordered my favorite roasted veggie sub on wheat with balsamic glaze and selected a bag of salt and vinegar potato chips and fresh-squeezed lemonade. Scott duplicated my order and we took our seats.

I noticed that Kyle kept looking at us throughout the meal; or rather, he was studying Scott with suspicion. I did find it curious that Kyle had thought that he recognized Scott, because it wasn't like there were a lot of men who looked similar to Scott. Maybe in Hollywood, but not in Pinewood Corners.

We had a pleasant lunch and talked about the upcoming ball. Scott wanted to know what colors he should wear to compliment my gown. I advised red and black, and Scott looked intrigued. He touched me a lot during lunch, resting his hand on my forearm or loosely holding my fingers in his. We left the restaurant and I was on cloud nine.

As we walked into the lobby of the inn, my cell phone began to ring. I dug it out from the depths of my purse and saw the number for the town council.

"Hello, Colleen, it's Jenny Mays from the Mayor's office? I wanted to see if you would be interested in riding on one of the floats in this year's Harvest Happenings Parade."

"Seriously?" I asked. I loved parades and never missed the opportunity to watch one. "Which float? Oh, it doesn't even matter, I would love to be in the parade!"

Jenny's warm chuckle reverberated over the line. "It's one of the three town merchant floats. You'll be able to promote your inn by dressing in period costume, and we'll put a banner with your inn's name on the float as well."

"That sounds wonderful, can I bring one of my dogs?" I gushed, then sobered as a thought hit me. "How long do I have to get a costume and everything?"

"Oh, plenty of time," Jenny assured me. "The parade is on Friday. As long as your dog is well-behaved, he's more than welcome. Glad to have you on board! I'll email you with the details." The line beeped and went silent.

Friday was five days away, and the ball was the following day. I had a lot to do in the coming week. I had to get my hair done, figure out which time period of the inn that I wanted to represent, find a costume, greet my first public guests, and get my employees into the groove of their new jobs. I really wished that I had a manager to rely on.

Scott sauntered into the room, coffee mug in hand. The man was a caffeine addict, all right. I beamed at him.

"You'll never guess who just called me! The town council wants to have me join the parade. Me! I've always wanted to be in a parade." I signed happily. "Hey, you should get up there with me! We could dress up in late 19th century costumes, and—"

"I don't think so," Scott interrupted me. My face fell.

"But why? I mean, I know you said you wanted to stay on and write a larger article. We're getting plenty of new bookings, but I can accommodate you, and it would be so fun to do this together."

"I'd really rather not. I don't like to be in the spotlight. I would rather just watch you shine up there on your own."

"But I would be happier with you next to me," I insisted. Scott's eyes took on that hardened glint that I had seen before.

His voice was rough around the edges when he snapped, "Colleen, I said that I'm not comfortable doing it. Just drop it, okay?"

"But I just thought—"

"Don't think. It won't work out well. I said drop it." His words were clipped and cold.

With that, he turned and stormed up the stairs, leaving me open mouthed and red-faced, humiliated by his rejection. *What the heck was that about?*

I meandered into the kitchen, thinking that I would grab a can of soda and think about the day's events. Just as I settled at the kitchen table, Jared burst through the back door.

"Good, you're back," he greeted me. He was wearing his old gray coveralls and a grimy backwards baseball cap that looked as if it had been red once upon a time. I noticed that he was carrying a small metal box, blackened with age or some other substance. He plunked the box down on the center of the table just as Pat walked into the room.

"Ew, get that off the table, it's filthy," I admonished Jared. "Or at least put something under it."

Jared responded by grabbing the notebook that I kept near the intercom and shoving it under the box.

"What have you got there?" Pat asked, adjusting her red framed glasses as she leaned over for a better look.

"Dunno," Jared replied. "I found it hidden behind the kitchen cabinets in the cottage. I demoed the cabinets and there was a hole in the wall behind them."

"What's in it?" I asked. Jared reiterated that he didn't know because he hadn't opened it yet. I picked it up gingerly and examined it.

"It's rusted shut, I think," I announced as I pulled ineffectually at the lid. Pat stepped up and pulled a tool out of her pocket. She held out her hand and I handed over the box. In a few tries, she had managed to pry the lid open. She peered at the contents.

"Papers. It looks like old letters or something," she reported, holding the box out to me. I took it and saw that there were indeed folded and crumbling papers stuffed inside. I pulled one of the squares out and gently unfolded it, trying to keep the decaying pages intact. Desiccated flower petals drifted out and disintegrated into bits. A memory triggered, of petals flying from the pages of a small red leather book … the memory slipped away and I shook it off.

"It's a letter," I said. I tried to make out the spidery, looping letters as I read haltingly aloud:

My Darling,

It has been only hours since I left you in our special place, and already I miss you fiercely. Until we are together again, I am only breathing and existing, anticipating when we are next able to meet, when I shall be once again fully alive and awake in your arms.

It pains me greatly to see you and to not run to you, to pretend that you are nothing to me, but I know that it must be so until we are ready to take our leap of faith and be together ever after. For now, we must keep our secret and I must play my role. But know, my darling, that I am always thinking of you and living for our next rendezvous.

Until then, my love, be well, and carry my heart in yours.

All my love, always,

S.

I looked up at Pat and Jared to gauge their reactions. Pat sat down at the table and began pawing through the rest of the papers in the box.

"There are dozens of letters in here," she said as she carefully unfolded another square and glanced at it. "They seem to be love letters. And I'd venture to guess that it was a forbidden love, or these letters wouldn't be hidden in a box in the wall behind the kitchen cabinets."

"Jared, did you just now find these?" I asked.

"Found 'em this morning. I tried to tell you, but you ran off to lunch."

I drew my shoulders up indignantly. "I did not 'run off,' I was invited to lunch and I went. I had no idea that you had found something like this." My feathers were definitely ruffled. "And it's an interesting piece of history, but no use to me. Maybe you should give them to Martin Weaver for the historical society archives."

Jared's face fell. "I thought maybe they had something to do with, uh, you know." He rolled his eyes toward the direction of the staircase and jerked his head toward Pat, who was still rummaging through the letters.

I raised my eyebrows and thrust my hands out, palms up. I had no idea what he was referring to or why he was being so mysterious.

Jared's face turned nearly purple as he gestured at the box, then at his pocket, then toward the kitchen door. I shook my head, still puzzled. He pulled the little notebook out of his pocket and waved it at me, and I finally understood that he was referring to the ghostly activity that he had been tracking with his journal. Apparently, he felt that the activity needed to be a secret between us and not let Pat know.

Pat looked up. "Do you think this has something to do with the paranormal stuff that's been happening?"

Jared's complexion went rapidly from purple to white, and I thought he might faint.

Chapter 10

Pat got Jared settled in one of the kitchen chairs while I got a glass of water for him. I explained that Pat was an experienced paranormal investigator and medium, and that she was here to help us. Jared's eyes were narrowed with suspicion, but he didn't protest Pat's involvement.

"What did you find out at the historical society this morning?" I asked her.

"Not too much that I didn't already know, beyond what you told me and my own online research," she said wryly. "I was hoping for something juicy like an old family cemetery or a murder on the property, but I didn't find anything about deaths on the property other than the tragedies that we know about."

She reached into the bag that she had hung off the back of her chair and pulled out a notebook. She flipped through the pages and cleared her throat. "We know about the death of the house's builder, Ezra McIntyre, in 1870," she began. Jared interrupted her.

"He didn't build the house, he commissioned builders."

"Of course," Pat agreed and continued. "And we know about the passing of Ezra's wife, Delia, and their stillborn son, whom they named Daniel, according to records. Those deaths likely occurred in the house as well, since home births were the most common back then."

She licked her finger and turned a page in her notebook. "Also the death of the eldest daughter of Walter Ellis in 1910, reportedly similar to Ezra's death." She paused and looked up from the page and met my eyes. "Her name was Sarah."

I jumped up from the table. "Sarah! You don't suppose that the 'S' signing off on these love letters was *that* 'S,' do you?"

"Could be, but I would hope we can get some further proof, like a handwriting sample known to be Sarah's that we could match or something like that."

"Oh, of course," I sat back down, deflated.

"Hey, kiddo, don't lose hope so quickly. We're just getting started here." Pat smiled at me reassuringly.

"Maybe the letters are to Sarah's fiance," I suggested. "Wasn't she distraught over being left at the altar?"

Pat flipped around in her notebook once more. "Yes, it was announced in the local newspaper, known at that time as the Pinewood Register. She was engaged to marry a gentleman named Calvin Hunnicut. The Hunnicuts were a very prominent family in the region in the early 1900s. Sarah was 16, and Calvin was 44."

I gasped involuntarily and Pat smiled sardonically. "That was not uncommon back then," she said.

"Child brides? I don't know why anyone is nostalgic about the so-called good old days." I was disgusted at the thought of such a young girl marrying someone nearly twice her age. "Why would her parents consent to it?"

"He was well off financially, and he came from a good family with a high social standing. I'm sure that they thought she had hit the jackpot. Back then, a woman's goal was marrying a man who was socially prominent and would be a good provider. Calvin checked all the boxes." She shrugged as if to say it was just the way it was.

I had no idea why I felt so upset at the idea of Sarah marrying Calvin. I wondered if the girl had had any say in the matter, or if old Calvin had just decided he wanted to marry her and Mr. Ellis had consented without bothering to consult his daughter.

"It does make sense that we assume that the weeping woman on the stairs is Sarah," Jared finally spoke up.

"I agree," Pat said. "I get the impression of great sorrow, but it doesn't take a psychic medium to understand that. You've heard the piteous weeping for yourselves."

"Would the historical society have any writings from Sarah?" I asked Pat.

"Possibly. Why don't we take these letters to Martin at the historical society and see what he thinks? I can ask him to make copies so that we can read them all without damaging them any further."

We all agreed that was the best course of action for now, and Pat would keep the letters safe in her room and take them to the historical society in the morning.

After Pat took the letters and went upstairs, Jared stood and began pacing. He was clearly agitated. Finally, I asked him what was on his mind.

"I don't know how to tell you this," he said, sitting back down. He took my hands gently in his. I was apprehensive. *Is he quitting on me? Is he ill? What's going on?* My mind whirled anxiously with possibilities, all of them negative.

"It's about Scott." I pulled my hands back and leaned away from Jared, crossing my arms over my chest.

"What about Scott?" I asked.

"I've been hearing things, like the fact that he's been asking several people in town for large amounts of money to 'invest' and I've had multiple people tell me how he's eating a bunch of meat even though he claims to be a vegetarian, and I've heard that he was unnecessarily rude to a lot of people, and his glasses aren't real, they're just clear blue-blockers."

"So you heard some small town gossip and just decided to run with it?" My voice shook as I tried to keep my building rage in check.

"I understand that you may not believe me, but it's people I trust telling me these things," he insisted.

"Like who?" I narrowed my eyes. My heart felt like it was being squeezed in my chest.

"Like Michael Brandon from the bakery, Miriam from the library, Kyle from Logan's, and Darlene from the El, to start with." Jared's pleading brown eyes didn't move me. I sat stubbornly with my arms still crossed. *He said something to Pat about investing just the other day.* I shook my head and looked away from Jared, not admitting my own thoughts aloud.

"I asked my brother, Brett, to run a check to investigate Scott's background."

I stood up so quickly that my chair nearly fell over. "You *what*!?" I slammed my palms down on the table top and leaned over Jared's shrinking form. "How dare you, Jared Baumgartner. My relationship with Scott is none of your business." I felt hot tears building and my face was on fire with indignation.

"I care about you—um, I mean, your safety. I don't want to see you getting hurt." Jared desperately reached out for me but I yanked away from him. His face fell. "Colleen, what do you really know about him? Where is he from? Who is his family? What's his history?"

"His family is gone, they died in a fire, have some compassion," I shouted.

Jared wrung his hands. "I'm only doing this because I care about what happens to you," he repeated.

"If you cared, you would be happy for me. A wonderful, gorgeous and successful man is finally interested in me, and you're just jealous that I found someone great." I bent down and looked directly into Jared's face. "You stop this so-called 'investigation' this instant. I don't want you around here if you're going to try and sabotage my relationship."

"What do you mean? What are you saying, Colleen?" Jared's eyes were so wide that I could see the whites all the way around the deep brown of his irises.

"I mean that I want you out of here. I'll find another contractor." I stood up straight with my shoulders back, arms crossed over my chest.

"Colleen, please, you don't understand. I have your best interests at heart. He's not behaving like the person he claims to be. I don't know what he's really after. You could be harmed," he pleaded.

The dark fury was filling me once again. I struggled to control myself. I wanted to reach out and slap Jared's face. My hands clenched into fists and I forced them to open as I gritted my teeth.

"He couldn't possibly be here just for plain and ugly me, isn't that what you're trying to say?" My face felt wet and I realized that angry hot tears were pouring down my cheeks. Jared's mouth opened, but I continued before he could reply.

"It's my life, Jared, and I'll be the one who decides whom I do and do not associate with, and whether or not I want to risk getting hurt. And I choose not to associate with *you*." I turned my back on him and pointed a shaking finger at the back door. "I mean it. Get out. Don't come back until you're ready to drop this nonsense and apologize to me, and to Scott."

I heard the scrape of the chair on the tile as Jared stood, followed by his footsteps that crossed the room. Finally, the back door opened and shut with a loud bang. I heard Jared's old truck roar to life and tear out of the driveway. I sank back down at the table, put my head down, and had myself a good, long cry. Lemon and Lime jumped onto the table and wove around me, head butting me, meowing softly, trying to comfort me.

I passed Pat on the stairs. She did a startled double-take at my red face and streaming eyes, but had the good grace to not say anything. I rushed up to my room and threw myself down on my bed, where I resumed my weep-fest. Bennie jumped onto the bed and leaned against my side, whining softly. I held his large, shaggy body and cried into his fur.

"Oh, Bennie, everything was going so well, and now it's all screwed up. Scott's mad because I asked him to be in the parade with me, and Jared … Jared is probably never going to speak to me again."

I glanced at the photo of my father on the nightstand, longing for one of his bear hugs that made everything seem okay. As I lay there, bawling my eyes out, I could've sworn that I felt a gentle hand stroking my hair.

*   *   *

I woke up in a darkened room. Bennie was gone, and I could hear the whispered patter of steady rain on the roof. I must have cried myself to sleep. I fumbled for my phone and discovered that it was after five in the evening. I sat up. My head felt like it was stuffed full of cotton after my cathartic crying, and I couldn't breathe through my clogged nostrils. I shuffled into the bathroom, turning on lamps as I went. The bathroom mirror confirmed that I looked as wretched as I felt. My hair was sticking up in unruly clumps, my skin looked red and blotchy, and my eyes were puffy and bloodshot.

After splashing cold water on my face, I turned on the bathtub faucet and plugged the drain and the tub began filling with water. I dumped in a good amount of jasmine scented bath gel, and the white mounds of bubbles began growing like tiny islands forming across the surface of the water. I inhaled the sweet floral scent and began to feel a bit better. A bath was just what I needed to clear my head.

I would have to find another contractor to finish the renovations on my cottage, and I would have to see about another on-call handyman. I soaked a washcloth in cold water to put over my eyes. I pushed those thoughts away for now and lowered myself into the warm and fragrant water and settled back with a deep sigh.

When I came downstairs, I saw that Pat was behind the lobby counter. I also saw a huge spray of red roses dotted with sprigs of baby's breath and fern fronds in a crystal vase sitting on the counter.

Pat looked up as I approached. "Feeling better?" she asked.

"Much," I replied with a small smile. "Who bought flowers? They're lovely." I leaned into the bouquet and inhaled the one-of-a-kind scent.

Pat pursed her lips and lifted one shoulder. "Read the card."

I fumbled the card out of the tiny envelope that was attached to a stake planted among the roses.

"Colleen, I am so sorry for being short with you this afternoon. You did not deserve to be treated that way. You are so special to me and I want to continue building our relationship. I hope that you will accept these roses as a token of my apology. Please forgive me. I'll see you in the morning."

My pulse quickened. I turned the card over. It was signed, *Yours, Scott.* For a split second, I felt a sliver of disappointment. Did I really think that a dozen red roses was Jared's style? Shaking it off, I shoved the card in my pocket. Pat was watching me intently.

"Good news?" she asked.

"You could say that," I replied, deciding that being vague was my best course of action. Pat didn't press for details.

"I hope you don't mind, but I took a couple of calls and answered some questions, and I booked in a couple for next week." Pat gestured at the computer. "You should really password protect this, or anyone will be able to get in."

"You don't have to do any work for me," I said.

"I've done a few stints working at hotels in various capacities, before I got into the paranormal business. That's why I decided to do a travel blog. I love traveling and staying at all kinds of hotels, motels, inns, and bed and breakfasts." Pat's long jet earrings dangled, reflecting the light.

"Thanks," I said. An idea began to grow in my mind. "Do you like Pinewood Corners, Pat?"

"Sure do. I feel so at home here. I've even been invited to become an official member of Darlene's poker club. This town is just the kind of place I've been searching for in my travels. It's small enough to be quaint, but large enough to have all the shops and amenities you need. The people are great, too. There's an overlying energy in town that just feels *good*. I could really see myself settling down in a town like this. I would have to find a job, and a place to stay," Pat mused, tilting her head thoughtfully to one side.

"How would you like to manage this inn? I had intended to find someone eventually, but I really need a reliable manager now. I like you and you have hospitality experience and you love the town and I know that paranormal stuff doesn't freak you out. You could stay here until you find a place." I snapped my fingers. "Wait, I'll bet my old house is still vacant. I'll call the landlord, Tammy Evans, and ask her if it's still available and see about setting up a tour for you. How about it?"

Pat's grin stretched wide, showing her long white teeth. "Actually, I have an alternate proposition."

I grinned back at her. "What did you have in mind?"

"I'm getting older, and I'm ready to settle down once and for all. But I don't just want a job, I want an investment for the future." She paused and adjusted her glasses. "I was thinking that if you're open to it, I could invest in the inn as part owner of the business, for a portion of the profits in exchange. I've got a nest egg that I've been hanging onto. We can have our attorneys hash the details out and make everything official." Pat's green eyes met mine. "What do you think?"

I considered Pat's offer. It would be wonderful to have another person to help run this inn with me. I still had high hopes of a future with Scott, but that was still a hypothetical daydream at this point, and I needed someone reliable right away.

Pat seemed ideal, with her grounded and cheerful energy. Having her as an investment partner could add another layer of security if I knew that she would always have the inn's best interests at heart.

I would need to contact Brett about the legal aspects, regardless of what I decided—shoot, was that okay, since I was on the outs with Jared? I supposed business was business after all. The idea of taking on Pat as a partner was intriguing, but it was too soon.

"I'll think about it," I said. "In the meantime, maybe you could start out as an assistant manager? I could have my attorney work up a contract for a salaried position for you. Once we get to know each other better, we can revisit the partnership idea. What do you say to that?"

Pat grasped my hand with her thin, strong one and shook it firmly. We sat there in a tableau, grinning at one another, for a minute.

"I think that sounds like a great plan," she said. "I accept the assistant manager position."

"Any online bookings?" I finally asked her.

"Not sure, I didn't check there. You'll have to show me the ropes with your software." Pat hauled herself out of the chair. "In the meantime, I stopped at the grocery store and picked up the ingredients for my famous vegetarian chili." She winked at me. "Join me for dinner in about an hour?"

I agreed enthusiastically and took Pat's place in the chair. I pulled up the online bookings and took care of confirming everything and then checked my email. One of the unread messages had a red exclamation mark next to it, meaning it was sent with high importance. I didn't recognize the sender's address. Warily, I clicked on the email and opened it.

Beware of Scott Carpenter. His name isn't Scott Carpenter. I haven't found his real name yet, but I'm on his trail. He isn't to be trusted, watch your back.

There was no signature. I closed the anonymous email and hit the delete icon in disgust. It was probably Jared, trying to butt into my budding relationship again. Really, he needed to get a grip.

At least things were on the mend with Scott. The note said that he would see me in the morning. I wondered briefly where he was, but tried to let it go. I wasn't his keeper, after all. I busied myself with clearing out the rest of my inbox and then checked for bookings on the website. The roses looked fetching on the counter with the flocked wallpaper and chandelier in the background, so I snapped a photo and posted it to the inn's social media site. By the time I was done, wonderfully rich aromas were drifting in from the kitchen.

"Mmm, that smells delicious!" I inhaled deeply and loudly through my nose and sighed in appreciation.

"Thanks," Pat replied. "This recipe won first runner up in a chili cook off in Sheboygan ten years ago." Her eyes took on a faraway look as the corners of her thin, expressive lips turned up. "Good times." She shook herself and focused on me. "It's just about ready, why don't you grab some bowls and pour us some milk?"

My stomach growled and I hurried to comply, setting out bowls, spoons, and glasses of cold milk. Pat carried the big red enameled cast iron Dutch oven with both oven-mitted hands and set it on the trivet in the center of the table. I could see at least three varieties of beans nestled in a rich tomato gravy dotted with herbs and aromatic pieces of onion. My mouth watered. Pat opened the oven door and pulled out a small baguette. I raised my eyebrows appreciatively.

"Wow, you baked bread?"

Pat laughed as she took off the oven mitts. "No, this is a take-and-bake loaf from the store, but it's nearly as good as homemade in my book."

"Hey, no complaints here," I assured her as I grabbed the tub of butter from the fridge.

For the first few minutes, we ate in silence, enjoying the wonderful food. Finally, I looked up from my bowl.

"Pat, this is delicious. You might give Mrs. Blake a run for her money."

Pat lowered her head modestly. "Oh, I doubt it. I can make a handful of really good things, but I'm not a well-versed cook." She tore off another chunk of the warm, pillowy bread and slathered it with butter. "Anything good happen today?" she asked before popping the morsel into her mouth.

"As a matter of fact, I was invited to be in the Harvest Happenings Festival's parade on Friday. They want me to ride on one of the merchant floats, in period costume."

Pat whistled. "Impressive," she said. "Where are you going to come up with a costume so quickly?"

I shifted in my seat. "That's a good question," I said. "There are some trunks up in the attic that I haven't explored yet, so maybe I can find something there that will at least inspire me."

Pat was staring speculatively at me. The older woman's seafoam-green eyes snapped with intelligence. "Are you going up there on the float alone, or bringing one of your employees?"

I looked down. "I asked Scott, but he's not really one for public displays," I explained, keeping my gaze glued to the table.

"Well, how about I go up there with you? I would love a chance to be in a parade. It's on my bucket list, you know. Along with skydiving and meeting Jeff Goldblum."

I finally looked up, a smile playing at the corners of my mouth. "Really?"

"Really. Let's clean up this mess and put our leftovers away and rummage around in the attic. I can't think of a better way to spend a rainy Sunday evening!" She rubbed her palms together in anticipation.

*   *   *

I followed Pat up the narrow staircase. The attic was lit with a series of bare bulbs hanging from the rafters on thin wires. The musty air in the attic smelled of camphor and dust and the undefinable smell of age.

The overhead lighting created sharp and outsized shadows. More than once, I had jumped at my own shadow or mistook the shadow of an innocent coat rack or dress form for a sinister entity when I had been up there furniture hunting.

I had neglected to look in the trunks, because I was only seeking household items and not clothes. The space extended over the entire west wing of the house. The air was chilly, and I wrapped my sweater more tightly around myself.

Pat wasted no time and marched directly to the nearest trunk. She dropped to her knees and opened the lid.

"Whew," she leaned back and fanned the air in front of her face. "Mothball city!" Undeterred, she dug into the piles of fabric. "Should've brought some gloves," she remarked as she extracted a crumpled and filthy calico apron.

We agreed to make three piles; yes, no, and maybe. The apron was tossed directly into the "no" pile. The first trunk yielded much of the same type of clothing, mostly dirty and damaged old things with no real value, which was probably why they were just shoved into a trunk, sprinkled with some mothballs, forgotten and left to rot from the ravages of time.

The second trunk looked more promising off the bat. The clothes were folded into parcels and wrapped in camphor-soaked oiled paper. Pat oohed and aahed over the lace and creamy cotton and linen creations, some entirely hand-stitched.

We giggled like schoolgirls over the snowy white bloomers and made ribald jokes. We also found a beautifully made day dress of black and white calico. Pat held it up. The puffy long sleeves narrowed at the wrist, and the bodice flowed into a narrow floor-length skirt.

"This is a possibility, especially if we find some hats," she said.

I eyed the creation. "Maybe for you. I need to find something that belonged to a woman who was a bit more full-figured."

Pat laid the calico dress carefully over an embroidered footstool. "That's a maybe, then." She continued burrowing through the trunk. She came up with a long black wool skirt and matching black peplum jacket with velvet-trimmed lapels.

"Hey, how about this? If we find a blouse—even a modern-day white blouse would do. This would fit." She held up the items and I grimaced.

"Great, I'll look ready for a funeral."

"Well, most clothes were dark back then. It was easier to keep clean." She put the clothing on the 'maybe' stool along with the calico dress. We also found a pretty day dress in a pale gray and another black skirt and jacket set as possibilities in the second trunk. The rest of the items were separated into piles. Pat insisted that vintage clothing and fabrics were valuable and we could sell to a collector or donate to the historical society. While Pat moved on to a third trunk, I took on the final one. I was inexplicably reluctant to lift the lid.

"Pat, look at this," I called to her. She looked up, her arms buried up to the elbows in piles of fabric.

"What's up?"

"This trunk is locked," I said, pointing to the rusted padlock dangling from the trunk's hasp.

"None of the others were locked. I wonder why?" Pat extracted herself from the clothes and came over. She examined the lock briefly and then stood and glanced around the room. Her gaze landed on a set of rusted fireplace tools. She grabbed the poker and before I could say a thing, she lifted the poker and brought it down on the padlock. It glanced off the lock and hit the floor, leaving a short, jagged scar in the wood.

"Sorry," she said, even as she was lifting the poker for another swing. This time, the poker hit the lock dead center and a few small sparks flew as the rusty lock busted and hung by its hasp from the trunk. "There you go," Pat said with satisfaction as she tossed the poker aside and removed what was left of the lock and lifted the lid.

A breeze ruffled my hair. *Where is the wind coming from?*

An explosion of creamy lace burst out of the top of the trunk. Pat gingerly lifted it up with her fingertips. "Whoo, this is beautiful!" she exclaimed as she shook the gown out. It was unquestioningly a wedding gown. "Do you think this was Sarah's?" she asked, echoing my own thoughts.

"If it was, she was a tiny thing." The dress was clearly made for a petite woman with a small waistline. "It could be …" I reached out tentatively to run my hand over the yellowing lace. "Ow!" An electric shock zapped my hand. I drew it back immediately and cradled it to my chest.

Pat gave me a quizzical look and set the gown aside. "There's a few more dresses, some lingerie … I think this was a trousseau."

"A what?"

"Back in those days, girls lived with their parents until their wedding day. When they got married, wealthier girls had a trousseau, which was a bunch of clothing items for their wedding and honeymoon. Adult clothes, since they were married women and needed to leave their youthful wardrobes behind.

Sometimes the trousseau also contained things for starting their household, like linens, dishes and serving ware, or items made by women in the family."

"Oh, that's interesting. What else is in there?" I peered into the space. Among the piles of fabrics, I spotted a flash of red. I pushed past the piles of clothing and linens and grabbed a small red leather bound book. As my hand closed around it, I felt that flash of deja vu, as if I had seen this book before.

I opened the cover and the first page stated "The Journal of Sarah Ellis." I held the open book up so that Pat could see it.

"Holy moly, it's Sarah's journal," she breathed. "We can compare the handwriting on the letters!" Pat leaped up from the floor and grabbed my hand. "Come on!"

"What about the clothes?" I asked as I was being dragged across the floorboards.

"We'll get them tomorrow," she replied.

Pat kept her room nice and neat. There were no piles of dirty clothes, and the bed was neatly made. I sat on the velvet covered bench at the foot of the bed while Pat got the box of letters and removed the one that we had already unfolded. She held the letter up to the randomly opened journal.

"Well I'll be. No question about it, the letters and the journal were composed by the same person. So we know that Sarah was canoodling with someone in secret." Pat began to pace back and forth, thinking out loud. "That likely means that her lover was probably considered unsuitable by her father. I wonder who he was?"

"She mentions seeing him every day, and not being able to show her feelings. Maybe a servant or something?"

Pat snapped her fingers. "Good guess. I did read a few other random letters, and they're all pretty much the same thing. 'My love, I live for the day we can be together, forever yours, blah blah blah.'"

I grinned. "You're such a hopeless romantic," I teased. "She was sixteen! You can't expect Shakespeare level prose."

I picked up the journal and flipped through it. The first pages were just musings of a teenage girl, passages about piano lessons and church picnics. I would have to read it more thoroughly to find out when our mystery man came on the scene. Maybe she would mention his name or give some clue as to who he was.

"Do you think that maybe that's why she's sticking around? Because she's still trying to reunite with her lover?"

"It's a possibility," Pat said, "Strong emotions can cause a spirit to linger."

"I'll take the journal to my room with me. It's not very big, I can probably skim through most of it before bed. Speaking of," I glanced at the clock on the mantle, "I should head to my room. I have staff coming bright and early tomorrow, and my first non-media guests checking in at 10:00."

I rose and, to my surprise, Pat enveloped me in a tight hug. I hugged her back, grateful for the older woman's presence in my life. It seemed impossible that we had only met last week. I had quickly come to rely on her support and her knowledge and experience. I knew that I craved a mother figure in my life, and Pat's kindness and generous spirit drew me to her.

"I'm going to let the dogs out for their last bathroom break, and then I'm turning in. Sleep well!" I left, taking the journal with me.

Chapter 11

The week proceeded in a blur of new guests checking in and working the kinks out with my new employees. Sandy Wilcox had come to me on her second day as housekeeper, upset because she felt that Eugenia Higgins was treating her as if she had never cleaned before and it was offending Sandy. I had to have a word with the older woman about allowing others to be competent in their own right and giving them the chance to succeed, and I reminded her that guidance didn't have to mean control. Once Eugenia lightened up and realized that some of Sandy's shortcuts were actually brilliant ways to save time without compromising on quality, she was a convert, and the women's relationship became more relaxed.

The guests raved about Mrs. Blake's cooking and the pastries from MB Squared. Everyone who had tried the spa services for themselves and their pets was pleased, and general feedback was positive.

Scott had formally apologized to me, and things were back on track with us. Jared continued to remain scarce, and

I didn't see him or hear from him during the week. I was surprised at the stab of disappointment that I felt each morning when I didn't see his beat up beige pickup truck parked on the side of the house. Jared had been a good friend and the loss of his presence left an empty spot in my heart.

I had, at Lacey's urging, made an appointment with Earlene Miller, my hairdresser at the Cut n' Style Salon, for hair extensions and highlights. I had never really paid much attention to my hair, but I really wanted to look amazing in the parade and for the ball.

This new interest in enhancing my appearance was fun, if a bit confusing at times. Earlene recommended tape-in hair extensions, which were pricey, but not as expensive as some other options. I elected for the half-head option, because I simply couldn't spare an entire day for the lengthy procedure of a full head of extensions.

As I settled into Earlene's chair, she whipped the leopard print nylon cape over me and fastened it behind my neck with a silver clip. "So, I heard you've been seeing an attractive new guy in town, that travel writer who looks like Superman."

I sighed internally, but I supposed that of all people, hairdressers were likely the most attuned to town gossip. "Oh, sort of. We've been hanging out, sharing a lot of meals, getting to know one another, that kind of thing," I replied, squinting as an errant spray of hot water hit my forehead and trickled down over my eyebrow.

Earlene expertly wiped it away with the tip of a towel and began massaging the citrus-scented foam over my scalp. I breathed deeply and closed my eyes, enjoying the invigorating smell of the shampoo—was that grapefruit? Earlene's fingertips scrubbed circles at my temples and I felt relaxed for the first time in ages.

"Well, I'm glad you met somebody, you deserve a good man. Although ..." she trailed off and focused on rinsing the foam from my hair.

"Although what?" I murmured, my eyes now closed as I relaxed and enjoyed the additional scalp massage that came with the application of the conditioning mask.

"I probably shouldn't say anything. A stylist is like a doctor," Earlene stated cryptically.

"How do you mean?"

"We know secrets. We know who colors their grays, who has a toupee, who has hair plugs, who has severe dandruff, stuff clients wouldn't want anyone else to know."

I was puzzled. "What does that have to do with me—or with Scott?" I asked.

Earlene's confidentiality apparently only went so far. She leaned forward and whispered into my ear, "He dyes his hair black. He came into the salon a couple days ago with light brown roots. Michelle did his touch-up. Shade 1V, Jet Black." Her head bobbed insistently up and down. "Makes you wonder what he's hiding."

"Really?" I kept my tone light and unconcerned. Come to think of it, I had never really noticed whether Scott's hair color was natural or not, but I supposed that men should be allowed a touch of vanity, too. After all, I was here to alter my appearance with highlights and extensions. Why should it be any different for Scott, just because he was a man? It didn't have to mean he was hiding anything, any more than I was hiding something by coloring my hair. If he thought his hair looked better jet black, more power to him. And the color really did suit him, contrasting so well with his blue eyes.

Nearly four hours later, I emerged from the salon with platinum-streaked hair that waved like a mermaid's and flowed well past my shoulders. The image of the woman reflected in the store windows as I walked down the sidewalk was a beautiful stranger.

I was wearing one of my new outfits that I had picked up while shopping with Lacey, a pair of dark washed boot cut jeans, chunky dark brown low-heeled ankle boots, a crisp white blouse and a camel-colored blazer. I had fought Lacey and won on browns and beiges versus pinks and greens. Lacey had been right about the shape of the bootcut jeans and fitted blazer being flattering to my figure, though.

I finally felt that my appearance fit the competent small-town business woman image that I wanted to project. Shoulders back and chin up, I confidently headed toward the municipal complex of Pinewood Corners to complete the most important errand on my list today.

"Hiya, Colleen," Mindy Cranston greeted me with a wide, vacuous smile. Her blonde hair was tall, her makeup heavy, and she could be a bit flighty but she usually meant well. She had been working at city hall for years as a dispatcher and receptionist.

"Hey, Mindy," I returned her greeting. "How's your family?"

"Oh, good, can't complain. How's business?"

"Can't complain." I grinned. "I'm getting steady bookings, even after the festival ends."

"I'm surprised that many people want to stay in a haunted house." Mindy shuddered. "Anyway, I'll let Martin know you're here."

I rolled my eyes and decided to let her remark go as she called Martin Weaver's extension. Martin was marrying Lacey in the spring. He and Lacey had met and fallen in love while pursuing the mystery of the town's famous lost necklace, which now belonged to me.

As the head of the historical society, Martin cataloged and curated all the documents and items. The museum was small but the collection was growing so much that Martin had applied for budgeting for an assistant curator and a larger space for the museum. The renowned necklace was a big draw for visitors.

Martin appeared disheveled. His shirt was half untucked and his nearly shoulder length wavy brown hair stood up in odd clumps, as if he had been running his hands through it. There was a dark blue blob of ink on the collar of his rumpled white button up shirt and the tip of his nose. I knew he also taught history at the local high school, which was currently on fall break.

"Hey, Colleen," he lifted a hand in greeting and gestured for me to follow him back to his office. He moved a stack of books and folders from the lone visitor's chair in his small and windowless office.

"Sorry, too many books and too little time," he apologized as I lowered myself into the chair. "Love the hair, by the way. Lacey told me you were having it done. It suits you."

"Thanks," I replied, ducking my head modestly. I felt a bit more confident lately, but I still had a long way to go. Martin settled into the high-backed swivel chair behind the desk and got right to the point.

"I read over the letters, and they are fascinating, but kind of repetitive. They're all about a series of secret rendezvous with her lover, who was apparently someone that her family didn't approve of."

He paused and handed me a manilla folder. "I made copies for you. The only identifiers she gives him are his physical attributes, which are rife with the purple prose of the day—his 'golden hair bright like the morning sun' or his 'eyes as blue and pure as the Lord's heaven.' She does at one point refer to him as 'L.' or possibly 'F.'—the handwriting isn't terribly clear. I imagine she wrote the notes quickly, and in secret. There are a handful of melodramatic love poems as well."

He glanced down, consulting his notes before he continued. "Their meeting spot seems to be a tree on the property, a large oak."

I gasped. "I know that tree, it's still there. Out by the groundskeeper's cottage. There are the most gorgeous primroses all around it."

Martin flipped a page and scanned over his notes. "This late in the season? Very intriguing. The disintegrating flower petals in the box with the letters seemed significant by their large number, so I asked Winona Flynn from the florist what she thought they were. She said they looked like primroses, so I looked up the meaning."

"You mean you looked up the varieties of flowers?" I asked, bewildered. Martin shook his head.

"During the Victorian era, floriography became very popular. It involved using the symbolism of various flowers to convey messages of love or friendship, or sometimes displeasure, with someone. It's also known as the language of flowers."

At my raised eyebrows, he explained further.

"For example, red roses mean love, yellow roses mean friendship. But the messages conveyed go much deeper." He reached across the cluttered surface of the desk and dug around in one of the piles of academic detritus and extracted a slim volume that he began to flip through.

"People back then would make these little hand-held bouquets, tied with ribbon, called 'tussie-mussies' and they would craft them with specific messages for the intended recipient in mind, based on the language of flowers. Tansy meant 'hostile thoughts' so you wouldn't include it in a bouquet for a lover, but you might if you were upset with someone and wanted them to know it. Violets stood for modesty and fidelity. Lily of the Valley meant a return to happiness. You get the idea."

"I'm beginning to," I said, brushing my newly long locks carefully over one shoulder. "So what do primroses mean?"

Martin flipped to a page in the book that had been marked with a pale blue sticky note. He ran his finger down the page and began to read aloud, "'These fiery blooms symbolize that kind of undying, all-consuming love that tells your lover you simply can't live without them.'" He closed the book and looked up at me, his amber eyes glowing under the harsh fluorescent overhead lighting.

I sat back and whistled. "Well, that sounds like a pretty intense affair." I dug around in my bag and produced Sarah's journal. "I found the journal of the eldest daughter of the house, Sarah, the one who was engaged and abandoned at the altar and, uh, died afterwards." I held the little red book out. "Interestingly, the same primrose petals are scattered throughout the pages."

Martin carefully took it and set it on the desk. "You know, despite the legends and rumors about her demise, Sarah's official—to use the term loosely—cause of death was listed as 'melancholy.' I suppose that was sufficient in those days to explain the death of such a young and apparently healthy person, especially if you wanted to dodge the stigma that the family would have faced at that time. I'm very curious about what her journal says."

"I read it. The book is only about half filled. There isn't much there. I think she was afraid her family would read the journal, so she kept things very light and on the surface. It's mostly filled with her daily mundane activities. You know, things like 'Today, I helped Mother make floral arrangements for the centerpieces for the dinner party and then took my piano lesson from Mrs. Gerber. Cook made stew and biscuits for supper,' stuff like that. She never writes about her lover. She does mention wedding preparations and says some things about how 'Father is excited for this match, he says it will secure his fortune.' She never indicates anything about being excited about getting married, and she never expressed any affection for her fiance, Calvin Hunnicut."

Martin rubbed his chin thoughtfully. "It does seem like the Ellis fortune declined after the death of Sarah," he mused. "I can't trace any deeds other than rental agreements in Pennsylvania after they abandoned the McIntyre mansion and left Pinewood Corners, so it seems that the family never owned another large property."

He tapped the red book. "May I take custody of this? Even everyday activities are fascinating pieces of history. I could work up a great display for the museum."

"Of course," I replied. I looked down at my lap and picked at imaginary fuzz on the leg of my jeans nervously. "I, um, also wanted to ask about something," I muttered, my voice barely above a whisper.

"What's that?" Martin asked without looking up as he shuffled the piles around on his desk. I didn't know if he was asking me to repeat myself or if he wanted to know my request, so I just blurted it out. I cleared my throat noisily, determined to sound confident.

"I want to wear the necklace, my necklace, to the ball on Saturday." The words came out in a garbled rush, but Martin understood what I had said. His head snapped up and his eyes were wide with alarm.

"You understand that it's a major security risk," he started to explain.

"But I will be able to wear it, if I want to, right?" I lifted my chin defiantly. After hesitating a few moments, he finally sighed and his shoulders slumped.

"Sure, it's technically yours, as you pointed out. I may need to check with the insurance company, as far as——"

"But the ball is in two days! I'm on a parade float tomorrow, and then Saturday is the ball ..." I was rambling in desperation, just like the old Colleen. "I got my hair done, and I went shopping with Lacey—it was the weekend that you were speaking at that conference—and I found the most beautiful dress, and it has red roses embroidered on it, and I think that means love, right? And I love this dress, and I know that the ruby necklace would look perfect and I really want to look good because I'm going with Scott, and he's definitely going to look amazing," I stopped to draw a breath.

Martin's lips quivered as if he was torn between laughter and frustration. "I'm sure that we can arrange for you to wear the necklace to the ball."

He held up one hand to stave off further verbal assault. "For a few hours, as long as you agree to return it the same evening and not have it unsecured in your home overnight."

He reached across the desk and placed a hand on my wrist, his eyes filled with concern. "There's also a personal risk to you, you know. That necklace is very valuable."

I sighed with relief. "Sure, of course, I totally get that. No problem, I'll be fine. I have a big, strong escort." I was nodding so hard that my new extensions were probably in danger of disconnecting.

Martin's face was set in a resigned scowl as he stood, ending our appointment. "I'll be in touch by tomorrow about the details of picking up and returning the necklace," he assured me as he opened the office door to usher me out. "Would you consider an armed escort?"

I stopped and turned around, frowning. "That would certainly cramp my style, Martin." I patted his shoulder. "Don't worry, I'll be fine," I repeated.

Another question occurred to me. "Do you know what ever happened to Sarah's fiance, Calvin Hunnicut?" I asked.

"He moved to the east coast and married a 17-year-old girl related to the Vanderbilts," Martin replied.

"Sounds about right," I groaned.

*   *   *

I headed to the Pinewood Washeteria, Dry Cleaning and Alterations, which was, to me, a very long and fancy name for a laundromat. Jessica Hayes, the woman who did all the alterations, was at the counter when I entered. I studied the way she had braided her long, chestnut hair in a French braid that wrapped around the side of her head and left a ponytail of loose waves cascading down one shoulder, contrasting with her vivid orange sweater. I would need to figure out new ways to style my own suddenly long hair now.

"Hi, Colleen," she called out cheerfully. "I think you'll be very pleased with how well your vintage items turned out."

I had dropped off the black and white calico dress and one of the black skirt and jacket sets that Pat and I had selected to wear in the parade. Pat and I had stood for measurements for the alterations while Jessica had oohed and aahed over the fine quality and hand construction of the old fabrics. We had ended up a captive audience for what turned into a lengthy lecture from Jessica about the evils of today's ubiquitous fast fashion.

Jessica disappeared into the back room and momentarily returned with the items wrapped in garment bags and hanging from wooden hangers. When I remarked on the hangers, Jessica's hazel eyes popped wide with indignation.

"I would *never* hang vintage clothes as well-made as these on a wire hanger!" she cried, her voice pitched high with outrage. This woman was definitely passionate about clothes. But when she peeled back the bags to display the dresses, I realized that it had been worth every moment of sitting through that lecture, because the clothes looked stunning, crisp and bright, as if they were almost new.

"Jessica, these look gorgeous. You did a phenomenal job!" I beamed at her. She beamed right back and handed me the invoice. My eyes bugged at the total, but she really had done a great job with the alterations and cleaning and repairs. I meekly handed over my debit card and thanked her for charging me an arm and a leg as I left with my prizes. I could hardly wait to get home and show Pat the outfits.

As I was backing out through the door, both hands full, I felt my body come into contact with a solid object. The object cried out indignantly, and I turned to find Rayna Reese standing in the doorway.

"Sorry," I muttered as Rayna stepped back onto the sidewalk. I wasn't surprised to see her here, since ninety percent of her wardrobe was probably dry clean only—a label I avoided like the plague.

"Excuse me," Rayna sputtered.

I wasn't sure if she was expressing the words to me or trying to correct my response. "I, uh, didn't see you there, excuse me." I attempted to walk around her on the sidewalk, but she stopped me, placing one slender white hand on my elbow.

Her sable bangs were artfully tousled under the brim of her red wool newsboy cap. Her violet eyes darted left and right as she licked her matte scarlet lips nervously.

"What's wrong?" I shifted the garment bags to one arm, probably crumpling and wrinkling them, but that was the least of my concerns right now.

Rayna looked positively paranoid. "I need to talk to you," she hissed in a stage whisper. I stared at her, waiting for her to go on, but she just kept glancing around, her chest rising and falling rapidly.

"About what?" I finally asked, because I couldn't stand the tension any longer. Rayna leaned forward, her warm, cinnamon-scented breath caressing my ear, giving me shivers.

"It's about Scott," she began. Her whisper broke off as I felt a presence step up behind me. I turned to see Scott standing there, looking quizzically at Rayna and I.

"Hello, ladies, what are you up to this fine day? Telling secrets?" His blue eyes flashed behind his glasses and his focus was on Rayna. His pinched face reminded me of the bitter, angry speech he had made earlier, ranting about Rayna and "her kind."

"Hi, Scott!" I blurted with false cheer. "I'm just out and about, running some errands. It's a busy week, you know, what with the new guests and settling in the crew, and the parade and the ball and everything. My goodness, the festival traffic in town this week doesn't help. It takes twice as long to get anywhere, even in little old Pinewood Corners, between all the activities like the daily pumpkin carving contest, and the dried leaf arts and crafts classes, and the pumpkin funnel cake booths everywhere, you just can't escape the crowds. Whoo!" I laughed nervously, patting my chest.

My attempt to diffuse the situation worked, but not in the way I had intended. Scott was no longer glaring at Rayna. Instead, they were both staring at me in bewilderment. Rayna began backing away.

"I have to get going," she murmured, her eyes shifting between Scott and me. She clearly mouthed the words *call me* in my direction right before she turned around and scuttled down the sidewalk. I had no earthly idea why she had not said the words aloud, since Scott was standing behind me and could clearly see her.

"Call her about what?" Scott's brow was raised.

Something about Rayna's behavior made me cautious. It was utterly unlike her to act like such a scared rabbit. She was typically the epitome of narcissism.

"Oh, nothing much. She just wants to schedule an interview about the parade and the inn. For the paper." I fibbed. The jury was still out on whether I would follow through to call her, though. She had acted bizarrely, but she was known to be dramatic, so it could be important, or it could be nothing.

"I'm glad I ran into you," Scott said. "I'm picking up my tux for Saturday, and I would love to grab some lunch with you, if you have time."

I grimaced. "I would love to, but I need to get back to the inn. Pat and I have to try on our dresses and make our banner for the parade float. Pat found some great hats and fancy folding hand fans in the attic to complete our outfits." I chuckled. "She's amazing. She even found a bow tie for Bennie to wear."

Scott's forehead wrinkled as he drew his thick brows together. "You're still set on having the dog on the float with you?"

"Of course." My voice rose with surprise. "The inn sets itself apart by catering to pet owners and their pets, so it makes sense," I insisted.

"Anyway," Scott said, his tone showing clearly that he was agreeing to disagree, "I'd better run to the menswear shop. We can have dinner together at the inn later." He leaned forward and gave the top of my head a brief brush with his lips before he turned away. He stopped and glanced back. "And your hair looks beautiful, by the way. You look like a goddess. I can't wait to see you in your gown for the ball." He pressed his pursed lips to his fingertips and blew me a kiss before striding away in the direction of Goddard's Menswear over on Willow Street.

I floated back to the lot where I had parked my car, on cloud nine. I had a very handsome and attentive man in my life—my boyfriend? Maybe. Scott and I hadn't discussed advancing our relationship to exclusive status yet. But we seemed to be headed in that direction.

I had financial security, I had pets that I treasured and a circle of friends. I owned the home of my childhood dreams, and my own business that was on track to be a success. I had found some great people to work for me, and I had found Pat. She had proven to be such a blessing, with her wisdom and humor. And having her managing the business with me as part owner had lifted a burden from my shoulders and made the responsibility of running the inn feel like a fun adventure. Pat had a way of making nearly everything feel that way, because she viewed the whole world as one amazing experience after another. The warmth of gratitude overflowed in my heart, and I pinched my upper arm. This life really was like a dream.

Chapter 12

"What do you think?" Pat simpered behind the black lace fan and twirled around. The black and white calico dress swirled around her ankles. She fluttered her eyelashes. I laughed.

"Excellent," I said. "You've nailed that 1890s look for sure, but I'm not that confident." I looked down at the black peplum jacket and with the leg o' mutton sleeves and the long black skirt. I felt like I was in mourning.

"Nonsense," Pat waved a hand at me. "You look like a very proper 19th century lady."

"Well, it's too late to find another outfit now, anyway, so I guess I'd better learn to love it," I said, smoothing the heavy skirt. "Let's get out of these clothes before we do something to mess them up. I'll meet you back here in ten," I told Pat.

When I returned to the lobby, Pat was already waiting. I leaned on the desk.

"Do you think the paint is dry on the banner yet?"

Pat went to the nearby table and gingerly touched her fingertips to the deep green letters sprawled across the white banner. "Feels dry to me," she reported, holding up her clean fingers. We rolled up the banner and stowed it in the back of my SUV for transporting to the parade in the morning.

Mrs. Blake had made a lovely meal of roasted chicken and mashed potatoes for the guests, and a vegetarian version with tofurky for Scott and me. Scott came down the stairs, sniffing the air appreciatively.

"Mmm, smells great," he remarked as his eyes settled on me. "What do you say to dinner in the east parlor?"

"I say that sounds wonderful," I replied. "Pat, would you like to join us?"

Pat looked uncharacteristically awkward, her eyes downcast as she murmured something about fixing a plate and taking it up to her room. I shrugged it off, figuring that maybe she was tired and a little anxious for tomorrow.

Scott insisted on getting our meals for us while I relaxed in the parlor. He had laid a fire in the fireplace and he set about lighting it as I settled on the couch with an ice cold Sprite in a wine glass.

"That feels great. It's the perfect ambiance," I sighed as I tucked my feet up onto the couch, curling up. The nights were growing colder and darker, and the fire was warm and cozy.

"Be right back with our dinner," Scott said, sketching a little bow before he left the room to head to the kitchen.

I sat sipping my soda and reflecting on my day. Lemon and Lime were both nestled down on the hearth rug, and Bennie and Ranger wandered into the room and lay down nearby, the flickering glow of the flames dancing over their fur.

The scene was so homey and pleasant that I impulsively grabbed my phone and snapped a photo of the animals sprawled in front of the fireplace and posted it to the inn's social media page with the caption "Furry friends and a fabulous fireplace = fall feels" and added the hashtag "cozyautumninn."

Just as I was placing my phone down, Scott entered the room with a tray covered by a silver cloche. The cloches had been Mrs. Blake's idea, to keep the food contained and warm if we needed to deliver it to the guest's rooms. I would never have dreamed of getting something so fancy, but they were great to have for serving the food and there was no denying that they looked elegant.

Scott set the tray on the coffee table and whipped the cloche off with a flourish to reveal two china plates filled with whipped potatoes swimming with silken vegetable-based gravy, green peas, and tofu dotted with herbs and spices. My mouth watered.

"That looks delicious. I really lucked out finding Mrs. Blake. Good thing that Jared—" I stopped short, my appetite suddenly sinking.

"For my lady," Scott said, handing me a linen napkin wrapped around a knife and fork. I smiled weakly and accepted the bundle, determined to forget about Jared for the moment and enjoy my dinner.

I tentatively dipped my fork into the potatoes and brought it to my lips. The potatoes were starchy and smooth and salty and the savory, rich gravy put them over the top. I rolled my eyes in ecstasy. My appetite came roaring back, and I plowed into the meal. Scott met me bite for bite, and we cleaned our plates quickly, much to the chagrin of the dogs, who had abandoned the hearth to sit and stare longingly at our dinner.

"I'm stuffed," I groaned, leaning back and clutching my stomach.

"I'll clear. Do you want dessert?" Scott popped up and began gathering up the plates and utensils.

I stared at him incredulously. "Are you kidding? After that gargantuan pile of food I just ate?"

"Mrs. Blake made chocolate cream pie," he taunted, wiggling his eyebrows.

"Maybe in a little while," I conceded. I held up my empty glass. "How about a refill? Or a cup of tea?"

"Your wish is my command," Scott replied, adding my glass to the dishes on the tray. "I'll be back with a pot of chamomile. You've got an early day tomorrow."

I snuggled into the sofa, pulling the afghan over my knees as I stared at the flames. I was full and content, warm and cozy, and my eyelids grew heavy. I was halfway dozing when a scream pierced the peace of the evening. I sat up abruptly, the afghan sliding to the floor. I blinked in confusion. Had I been dreaming? The cats had scattered and the dogs were at the doorway, whining anxiously. Bennie let out a short, sharp bark.

"What's wrong, boy?" I stood and patted the back of the dog's head. I was almost convinced it was a dream, when a woman's voice called out for help. I took off running in the direction of the voice.

I skidded into Scott, running in the same direction. His eyes were wild with panic as he clutched my shoulders.

"What's going on? Was that a scream?"

I pulled away from him and kept going. "I think so," I said.

I ran toward the staircase to find one of the guests, Mrs. Burton, sitting on the landing and looking dazed. My chest clutched.

"Did you fall? What happened?" I looked at Scott. "Call 911!" I cried.

"No, no, it's all right, I'm not physically hurt," Mrs. Burton said, stopping Scott as he was pulling out his phone. I didn't like the way she had put emphasis on the word "physically."

"What happened?" I asked again, as I sank down on the landing next to her. She brushed her long white hair back with a shaky hand.

"I don't know. I was coming down to get another serving of that pie, and some coffee, when …" She stopped and seemed to be searching for the right words.

"When what?" I prodded gently for her to continue. I saw Pat's silhouette at the top of the stairs.

"Everybody okay?" she asked.

"Mrs. Burton was just coming down for some dessert and coffee," I explained. "But then something happened, right?" I nodded at Mrs. Burton to continue.

"Well it just sounds so silly to say it out loud," she laughed shakily.

"Maybe it's silly, but maybe it's not," Pat said as she made her way down to the landing, settling on Mrs. Burton's other side. Scott remained at the bottom of the stairs, his blue eyes wide.

"I was halfway down the stairs," Mrs. Burton gestured at the landing. "And all of a sudden, a man appeared right in front of me. He was very agitated, waving his arms and shouting wordlessly, pointing to the bottom of the stairs. I screamed, and he … he vanished. Then I called for help." She shrugged helplessly, her cheeks reddening.

Pat whipped out her phone and opened an app and began taking notes.

"What did he look like?" she asked briskly.

"Um, he was a man, like I said. He looked upset." Mrs. Burton wrung her hands together.

"Did he have a hat? Facial hair? Glasses? Was he dressed in modern or old fashioned clothes?" Pat asked in a matter-of-fact tone. *Smart, she's being very down to earth and asking mundane questions to calm Mrs. Burton down and get her focused.*

Mrs. Burton closed her eyes. "He had a flowing mustache, like in the old-time pictures. He was wearing round wire-framed glasses and some kind of suit, with a vest. It looked like an old-timey suit, with pinstripes." Her eyes popped open and she took a shuddering breath. "It really scared me."

Pat gave her a one-armed hug. "Of course it did. Why don't I join you in the kitchen for some coffee and pie?" She took Mrs. Burton's elbow and guided her down the stairs and to the kitchen, shooting a significant look at me over her shoulder, as if to say, "We need to talk about this later."

Scott was frowning. "You have got to be kidding me," he said, his voice gruff with disbelief.

"About what?" I asked, descending the stairs to meet him.

"About that lady having hallucinations. You should take her to the hospital."

"Scott, about that," I began. I wasn't sure how to go into it, so I just plunged ahead. "Some odd things have been going on in the house, and Pat is helping figure it all out. She has a background and experience with these things."

"Odd things? What are you trying to say?" Scott's handsome features were distorted by his scowl.

"Paranormal type things," I said, and Scott absolutely exploded.

"What?" he shouted, throwing his hands up in the air. "That's impossible, because those things don't exist!" He began pacing the hallway.

"But Pat says—"

Scott turned and in two long strides, he was directly in front of my face. He leaned forward, his face inches from mine.

"Pat," he growled through his teeth, "is trying to gain your trust with her woo-woo gibberish. She's a charlatan, and you're actually going to stand here and tell me that you believe in all this—this junk?"

I swallowed hard, my mouth suddenly bone dry. I retreated a few steps until my back touched the wall.

"Scott, I've had experiences, too, and I do think something beyond the ordinary is going on here."

Scott closed his eyes and took a deep breath. He released it slowly, and his posture relaxed. He met my eyes and we stood like that for an intense moment.

"Okay," he finally said. "I can accept that you think you're experiencing something. But I don't subscribe to such beliefs, and I would ask that you not give Pat such blind trust in these matters."

My stomach roiled and I fervently wished that I hadn't eaten so much food so recently. I waited a moment for my stomach to make up its mind, and the food finally settled.

"I can live with that. For now." I smiled weakly at Scott and he opened his arms. I walked into them, taking in his warm and spicy cologne and the softness of his shirt against my cheek as he hugged and rocked me.

"I've changed my mind about dessert. I'm going up to bed," Scott said, pulling gently away but keeping a gentle grasp on my shoulders. "Are you going to be okay?"

"I'm fine. I'll be going up shortly myself. I have to be up before dawn to get myself into costume and do my hair for the parade." I tried to give Scott a reassuring smile. He squeezed my shoulders and ran his hands down my arms, ending with a brief kiss pressed to the backs of my hands.

"Good night, then. Sweet dreams." He waggled his fingers at me as he left the room.

As I was folding the afghan, Pat poked her head into the room.

"I got Mrs. Burton calmed down. I think maybe she saw old Ezra," she reported. She came into the room and I noticed that she was clutching a notepad and several yellow pencils.

"Catching up on your correspondence?" I joked.

"Not exactly," she replied, setting the pad and pencils on the coffee table. "I thought we might try some automatic writing. I'd really like to know what these spirits want, and why they're hanging around."

I concentrated on folding the afghan, aligning the corners and smoothing the edges. After a few moments, I finally said, "I've heard of that. Isn't it when you sit with a pencil and paper and let spirits use your hand to write?"

"Pretty much," Pat said, settling down on the sofa. I picked up the poker and shifted the glowing logs around.

"I don't know. Does that mean that the spirits possess you?" I asked anxiously.

"Not the way you're thinking," Pat assured me. "You're opening to hear messages, but they don't take over your physical body or anything like that."

She picked up one of the pencils and flipped the pad open to a blank page. "I'll do the honors. I've done it before, but of course, Nat was way better at it. I really miss her."

She poked a finger under her glasses and dabbed her eyes. She cleared her throat and sat up straighter. "Okay, enough of that. Have a seat, and we'll get going."

I sat down in the wing chair next to the couch. I was apprehensive but I had to admit that I was intrigued. Pat settled back with the pad in her lap and the pencil held loosely in her right hand, the tip resting on the paper. She began taking deep, even breaths with her eyes closed.

I stayed silent, watching and waiting. Soon, Pat's breathing became so even that I was afraid that she had fallen asleep, but suddenly her hand began to move, and I could hear the scratching of the lead across the paper. I was a bit disappointed. I had expected a bit more drama, like some sort of boom or voice or a strong scent or something. I really had read too many romance novels.

Pat's hand scribbled away, while her eyes remained closed and her posture relaxed. I wondered nervously how long I should wait. Should I wake her? Was that bad, like waking a sleepwalker? My hands twisted in my lap anxiously. The clock on the mantel struck just as the doorbell rang. Pat's eyes flew open. The door chimes rang again, and the caller began pounding on the door.

"Good gracious, we'd better see who that is. It sounds urgent," Pat remarked blithely as she set the pad and pencil down and rose from the couch.

I glanced longingly at the notepad, which was covered in scrawl, but followed Pat to the front door. There was a man and a woman with two girls on my front porch.

The man spoke first. He was wearing thick glasses and had a receding hairline.

"I'm so sorry to disturb you so late in the evening," he began. Then one of the girls, the taller one, piped in.

"I saw your post from tonight," she blurted out. "You've got our Snowball!"

"Your what?" I asked, bewildered. The girl opened her mouth to speak but she was interrupted by a flurry of barking accompanied by a scrabbling of claws on hardwood. Bennie, Mac, and Ranger came barreling into the foyer. Ranger shot out from the group and, before I could stop her, she ran between my legs and into the arms of the girl who had been speaking.

"Snowball!" the girl cried rapturously, gathering the little white dog up into her arms. The family encircled her, all of them hugging around the dog with cries of joy. The dog was ecstatic, wiggling and wagging and trying to lick all of their faces at once.

"What's this?" Scott appeared at the foot of the staircase.

The man stood and held out his hand. His brown eyes were shining with tears behind his glasses.

"I'm Doug Emmans. Thank you for finding Snowball and taking good care of her," he said. Scott looked at Doug's hand as if it was a particularly slimy slug.

"I'm sure I don't know what you're talking about. This is my dog, Ranger. I've had her since she was small." He snapped his fingers and pursed his lips in a short, sharp whistle. "Ranger, come!" The dog paid no attention whatsoever and continued to bask in the rapture of the family's embraces.

The man who had introduced himself as Doug Emmans reached into his back pocket and took out his wallet.

"Here you go, the fifty dollar reward," he held a handful of bills out to Scott. Scott hesitated, watching the dog interact with the family. The smaller girl smiled broadly at him. Her face was wet with joyful tears, and she had a gap where her baby tooth had fallen out.

"Thank you, mister," she said, her voice thick with emotion.

Scott reached out and gingerly took the money that Doug held out.

"Well, it seems that your girls will be heartbroken if I insist, and since I'm not a breaker of little girls' hearts, I'll go along to get along," he said, shoving the money into his front pocket.

"But wait, if that's your dog—" I began.

Scott shook his head and pulled at my elbow. "It's all right, you can see how much these people love her." He finally held out his hand and shook Doug's. "Take good care of her," he admonished.

"Sure, of course we will," Doug replied, gathering up his family and herding them off the porch and down the walk. "Thanks again," he called out with a wave as they all piled into a silver minivan. I turned to Scott.

"What a selfless thing that you did, giving your beloved dog away to make those children happy," I told him.

He shrugged it off. "It was the only thing to do. They lost their pet, and they thought they found her. I couldn't crush their hopes." He tilted his head to the side. "How did they know to come looking for her here?" My eyes grew wide at the realization of what I had done.

"I posted a picture of her on social media, it was her and Bennie and Lemon and Lime all lined up in front of the fireplace, on the inn's account," I said, realizing that it was probably my fault that Scott had lost his dog. "I just thought it was a cute photo, I had no idea that this would happen," I began to explain, but Scott cut me off with a gentle finger to my lips.

"Shh, it's all right. I'm happy that those girls are happy. They can go to bed tonight happy and content, and not worried about their lost pet for the first time in who knows how long, and I'm fine with that."

I felt warm and gooey inside over how beautiful Scott's gesture was, and I beamed at him proudly.

"You shouldn't have taken the reward money if you wanted to make a selfless gesture," Pat remarked. It was like a bucket of cold water thrown over my warm fuzzies.

Scott narrowed his eyes at her and said, "Anyway, I have some work to do before I turn in for the night, so I'll be seeing you in the morning. Good night." He turned and headed back toward the stairs.

Pat and I stood like statues, waiting until Scott's footfalls faded down the upstairs hall. Then, we practically shoved each other down trying to run to the parlor and retrieve the notepad. Pat picked up the notepad and squinted at the page.

"I can barely read this scrawl," she complained. I glanced over her shoulder. The writing was indeed sloppy, with some of the letters looping and large and some cramped and tight, and the lines sprawled in all directions with a total disregard for the lines on the paper.

"It looks like a couple of words appear quite a bit," Pat said, her nose almost touching the pad. "I can see 'fell, gossip, false' over and over." She looked up from the paper, her green eyes wide. "Do you think old Ezra didn't hang himself after all, that he actually fell and it was some kind of accident?"

Before I could reply, a candlestick flew from the mantle and crashed into the wall behind the couch. I squealed in surprise and clutched my throat.

Pat glanced upwards. "Is that you, Ezra? Do you want the world to know that you didn't commit suicide, that your death was an accident?"

The candlestick that had hit the wall came rolling out from under the couch and hit the side of my foot.

"Thank you, Ezra," Pat responded. "We'll do our best to get the truth out there, if you'll stop terrorizing our guests by appearing to them."

The lights dimmed, flickered, and brightened.

"Deal," Pat said with a short laugh.

"How are you so calm about all of this?" I whispered fiercely.

"It's not my first rodeo," she replied as she bent to gather the pencils. She straightened up and closed the notepad. "I think we've seen that last of Ezra for a while. We'll have to investigate a bit further, but if he really did die in an accident, we can find a way to let the world know."

She glanced at the clock on the mantle. "For now, I'd better mosey along to bed. See you bright and early!"

With that, she marched out of the room, leaving me open mouthed. With a shrug, I picked up the candlestick, replaced it on the mantle, banked down the fire, and headed upstairs to try and get some sleep before my big day tomorrow.

*   *   *

"Did you remember the hat boxes? And the banner?" I asked anxiously as I pulled out onto the road.

"Of course, I had that checklist you gave me," Pat replied crossly.

"Sorry, I just want everything to be perfect," I said.

"Perfection is a cruel illusion," Pat retorted.

I flipped on my turn signal with a sigh. "You know what I meant. It's my first parade." I wanted to represent the inn in the best possible light.

"I know," Pat said, returning abruptly to her usual sunny self. "I just want you to lighten up a little and enjoy the moment." She reached into the back seat and adjusted Bennie's bow tie and stroked his ears. His tail thumped on the seat.

"I'm so nervous. What if I have a wardrobe malfunction up there, or what if I fall off the float and hurt and humiliate myself?" I clutched the wheel.

"What if pink monkeys fly out of your ears?" Pat interjected. "You'll be fine. Here we are."

I had almost missed the turn into the parking area. I slammed on the brakes and we all slid sideways as I whipped the vehicle into the sudden turn. As I drove through the rapidly filling lot, my thoughts returned to the automatic writing session and Ezra's anxious messages.

"What do you think Ezra was so agitated about last night?" I gritted my teeth as I clutched the steering wheel.

"Maybe he's still grieving his wife's death, maybe he's still angry at his daughter, depending on whether it's Ezra or Mr. Ellis," Pat said as I eased the SUV into a parking spot. Before I could respond, she was hopping out and opening the back to grab Bennie's leash.

We were already dressed in our costumes. My hair had been teased within an inch of its life into a Gibson Girl style pompadour at the front, with fat curls draping down my back. I felt silly, but it was appropriate for the period and once I pinned my hat on, it would look better. I had wanted to put the hats on before we left, but Pat had wisely pointed out that we would not fit inside the low ceilinged vehicle with them on.

Now, we used the windows of the SUV as mirrors while we helped one another get the massively wide brimmed hats on. Pat had tracked down some of the massive and frighteningly long hat pins in one of the local antique shops. I had to admit that we looked very authentic to the time period.

We made our way to the designated area where the floats were lined up, ready to wind their way along the designated parade route. In the distance, I could see the lawn chairs lined up along the street, holding places for eager parade goers who had placed them there the night before.

Jenny trotted up as soon as she saw us, clipboard in hand.

"Very nice," she purred as she studied our outfits. "You both look great. Where's your banner?"

I handed over the rolled-up canvas and she shouted to a tall, stocky man walking past and tossed it to him. "Float seventeen," she called as he caught the bundle. Jenny turned to us.

"Your float is second to last. The final float is the mayor's horse-drawn carriage, and that closes out the parade. As you know, this year's parade theme is 'Pinewood Corners Through the Ages.' We're starting with the modern day, and working our way back. You're the founding float, so keep big smiles on your faces, and keep waving."

She pointed to a long table nearby. "Go check in with Freddy, and he'll give you your favors. Toss them out to the crowd. Aim low so you don't hit anybody in the face, and aim mostly at the kids, and be sure to portion them out so you don't run out before the end of the route. Make your way over there after."

She pointed toward the row of floats. "Tell them you're on float seventeen, and a volunteer will help get you up there."

I was about to ask a question about how to portion the items, but Jenny's name was called from somewhere and she jogged off. I turned to Pat.

"Well, I guess we should get our favors, whatever those are." I pointed to the table Jenny had indicated. The favors turned out to be a bucket filled with shiny wrapped candies, tiny plastic toys, and strands of beads. Now I understood why we had been told to aim at the kids.

Riding the float was amazing. I could feel the energy from the excited throngs of people that waved and whooped and cheered. The breeze grabbed my hat, and I was glad for the terrifyingly long hat pins holding it on.

Bennie was nervous when the float began to move, but he calmed down quickly and the crowd was delighted to see him. Pat had the time of her life, hamming it up, waving to the spectators and dancing to the Pinewood High Marching Band and tossing favors into the crowd.

The mayor's carriage, pulled by two gorgeous white horses, trailed along behind us and we could see Mayor Reese, with Rayna beside him, waving and smiling. The mayor wore a formal suit from the turn of the last century, with top hat, tails, and all. Rayna was radiant in a stunning lavender gown suitable for a top-tier debutante ball.

At one point, I caught a glimpse of Scott's handsome form in the crowd. He was beaming and waving at me. I tossed a string of beads his way, but I didn't see if he caught them.

We cruised along the parade route and my bucket of favors was almost empty. Luckily, the route was almost ending. Once we turned off onto Oak, we would be headed around to the stopping point. I grabbed the final handful of toys and beads and flung them into the crowd all at once, and the children scrambled to gather them up, screaming with laughter.

"Whoo, that was an absolute blast," Pat remarked. Her cheeks were flushed with the cool breeze and her eyes shone with excitement. The float coasted to a stop and Pat unhesitatingly leaped into the arms of Michael Brandon, who had been two floats up with Mikki, riding a giant cookie shaped float. Michael caught her tall, slim form without apparent effort. He set her on her feet with a grin.

"Nice outfit, Lady Chatterly," he remarked.

"I'll take that as a complement, since she was quite scandalous for her time," Pat replied, hands on her hips. "The book was banned in multiple countries, you know. Society had a tizzy over an explicit affair between an upper-class woman and a working class man. And thanks for the assist. I never pass up a chance to jump into the arms of a beautiful man."

Michael blushed and held up his hands to me. "You look lovely, too. Very authentic," he told me.

"Thanks. Could you grab Bennie?" Once I was back on solid ground, I remarked, "That was so much fun, wasn't it?"

"Sure was, and Mikki looked so adorable," Michael glanced in the direction where his girlfriend was standing and chatting with Mayor Reese, and he smiled warmly. Mikki was dressed as one of the Keebler Elves—round wire-framed glasses, pointed ears, pointy hat and all.

"There's no better way to dress when you're on a float that looks like a cookie," I said and Michael chuckled. He was wearing a far more pedestrian outfit, jeans and a t-shirt and apron with his bakery logo.

"Her grandma Jo made the outfit, she insisted that Mikki had to be a Keebler Elf in the parade. And when Jo Weaver insists, she gets her way." Michael's voice was tinged with admiration. Mikki's grandmother was definitely a force to be reckoned with.

I glanced over Michael's shoulder and saw Jared approaching purposefully. "Well, gotta get going," I told Michael. "See you later." I tugged at Bennie's leash and grabbed Pat's arm as we passed. "C'mon," I said, hurrying her along.

"Jiminy Christmas, what's up with you?" Pat demanded as she was dragged to the car. I didn't waste time responding, I just opened the doors and got Bennie and myself inside as quickly as possible. I realized immediately that Pat was right, the hats wouldn't fit under the low roof. I slouched down in my seat.

"Get in, what's taking you so long?" I hissed.

"Let me get this monster of a hat off," she grumbled as she climbed into the passenger seat. "My goodness, I can't imagine being expected to wear something like this every time I left the house." She tossed the hat into the back seat next to Bennie and settled back with a sigh. "That was an unforgettable experience. Definitely one for the books." She waited until I had guided the SUV out of the lot and onto the road before she continued.

"So why did you hustle me out of there so fast? Was it because of Jared?"

I flipped my turn signal on and coasted up to the red light.

"Honestly?" I turned and looked directly at Pat. "I didn't want to confront Jared right now. He's cooked up some wild idea that Scott isn't who he says he is, or some such nonsense." The light turned green and I pulled forward. "He tried to hire his lawyer brother to investigate Scott's background, if you can believe that," I scoffed.

Pat was uncharacteristically silent for several minutes. Finally, she changed the subject by asking about my plans for the rest of the day.

"I'm going to practice my hair and makeup for the ball," I told her. "I'm not great at that stuff, obviously."

"Oh, I think you're pretty good. And I'm happy to help. I'm going to the ball with Darlene and her poker club. We're going as the Cougar Brigade," she laughed.

I was confused, and I said as much.

"You know, because we're all ladies of a certain age, and we're single, so we're cougars," she explained. I snorted with laughter.

"Pat, I'm glad I met you," I told her.

"Right back at you, kiddo," she replied.

Chapter 13

As I exited the municipal building with my package, I felt like there was a giant target painted across my back. I clutched my tote bag and told myself to relax. There were only a handful of people who knew that I was taking the ruby necklace out of the museum, including the mayor, Martin Weaver, the insurance company, and the security guard. I hadn't even told Scott or Pat. I wanted to surprise everyone.

I consciously slowed my pace and forced myself to walk in a leisurely fashion to my SUV and climb in like a normal person, rather than flying in screaming like a banshee and roaring off down the road. I started the engine and drove sedately out of the lot.

I wanted to stop off at the drugstore for some false eyelashes to complete my look, but didn't dare go anywhere but straight home with the necklace. I would just have to hope that a couple of coats of mascara would be sufficient. I glanced at the tote bag on the seat beside me. I doubted anyone would be looking at my eyes anyway, not with that stunning ruby glimmering at my throat.

I went directly to my bedroom and stashed the jewelry case under my pillow, as was my habit when I was trying to keep something safe. Logically, I knew it was ridiculous, but emotionally, it made sense to me. After showering and slathering myself with jasmine-scented body lotion, I strapped myself into my foundation garments, wrapped my hair in a towel, slipped into a pink and gray plaid robe and went in search of Pat. She was in her room, getting ready.

"I'll be done in a jiffy," she explained, "that's why I like my hair short, it's quick. And my makeup is lipstick and mascara, easy-peasy," she grinned. "Now, for a lovely young thing like you, we can go all out." She rubbed her hands together and gave her best villainous laugh, "Bwah-hah-hah-ha!"

I burst out giggling and handed over my cosmetics bag.

An hour later, I was staring at a version of myself that I had never seen before. I had always thought of myself as average on a good day, but Pat had worked magic with her makeup and hair talents.

"I worked behind the scenes at a beauty pageant one summer," she confessed. I wondered what this woman hadn't done, besides skydiving and meeting Jeff Goldblum.

My eyes seemed bluer and wider, the deep black lashes fanning out coquettishly. My brows were shaped into perfect arches and brushed neatly into place. My lips looked fuller, thanks to the expert lining Pat had applied, and they shimmered with the plush red lipstick and gloss laid over the top.

I had actual cheekbones somehow, and my hair was halfway up, the braided top half circling my head like a tiara while the bottom shimmered in romantic waves down my back.

"Pat, this is amazing, I can't believe what a good job you did," I said, staring at my image in the mirror. "I don't even look like myself."

"You look like a nicer version of yourself," Pat told me, patting my shoulder. "You're a very lovely woman."

Glossing over her comment, I thanked her and excused myself to go and get dressed. I took my gown out of the garment bag and stepped into it, carefully pulling it up over my hips and shoulders. I tried in vain to get the back fastened, but after I started to get sweaty, I gave up. I was reluctant to mess up the expert makeup that Pat had applied. I would have to ask for help. I didn't want Scott to see me until I was in my full regalia. We had agreed to meet in the lobby at six. Pat gladly obliged, helping me with the fasteners.

"Wow, that is one beautiful dress," she remarked. "It's very flattering on you."

"Thanks, I love your gown, too," I replied. Pat was wearing a silver lamé sheath dress that complimented her tall, slim frame.

"Thanks, I love wearing anything metallic. By the way, I contacted Martin Weaver about Ezra McIntyre's death. He's going to look into it," Pat said. "That is one sharp man. If anyone can get to the bottom of things, he can."

I smiled. "Martin would be flattered to hear you say that." I twirled in front of the mirror. In the black off-the-shoulder gown, with the blood-red roses and emerald vines spilling down the bodice and flowing down onto the skirt, I looked like some sort of gothic princess. It was a totally new look for me, and I loved it.

"I just need to grab one more thing, and I'm ready to go," I told Pat. I hurried down that hall to my room, closing the door behind me. I slid the midnight blue velvet jewelry case out from under my pillow and lifted the lid with shaking hands.

The 15 carat heart-shaped ruby nestled in the velvet pillow of the case glittered like holy fire, greedily capturing every bit of light that touched it. I took a deep breath to try to calm down enough to pick up the necklace and fasten it around my neck. It was heavier than I expected. Its weight reinforced how rare and valuable this piece of history was. As I fastened the catch at the nape of my neck, the ruby settled into place just below the hollow in the center of my collarbones.

My ancestress had never had the chance to wear the necklace and I sobered for a moment, thinking of her, and of my lineage. I had always felt very alone in the world since my father had died. I lifted the frame containing the photo of my father and me from the dresser and gazed lovingly at it.

"Thank you for being my father, even if we only had a short time together on this earth," I whispered, lightly brushing my lips across the image of his smiling face. "Thank you for leaving me this legacy." I blinked back tears as I replaced the photo on the dresser.

I took one last look at myself in the mirror. I had been correct. Nothing else mattered— not the hair, the makeup, or even the elaborate gown. The ruby necklace shone like the sunrise and eclipsed everything else. I would definitely sparkle at the ball tonight. I noticed that it was a few minutes past six.

I grabbed my tiny clutch purse, making sure that my lipstick and powder were inside for touch ups. I tried to cram my phone into the tiny bag, but the clasp wouldn't close no matter how I arranged the phone, so I reluctantly left it on the dresser. I snatched my black velvet mask from where it hung on the corner of the mirror and tied it on.

I hoped that tonight would solidify my budding relationship with Scott and plant the seeds for something real and permanent to grow. I wondered briefly whether Jared would be at the ball, but discarded the thought. Everyone went to the Harvest Moon Ball.

The shops and businesses in Pinewood Corners all closed down early so that the business owners and employees could attend. I had given all my own staff the evening off as well. I squared my shoulders and determined that if I ran into Jared, I would just have to deal with him. Really, his obsession with Scott was completely uncalled for.

I glided down the staircase and felt the hair on my forearms stand up as I passed the icy cold spot on the landing. "Come on, Sarah, give me a break for once," I whispered, and to my amazement, the chill abruptly dissipated. I clutched the railing, unsteady in my heels and unable to see well with the mask on. I was focused on getting safely to the bottom of the staircase and I was startled by a loud wolf whistle.

"You look …" Scott's jaw was hanging open. He wore a gorgeous tuxedo with a red bowtie that matched the roses on my dress. The black mask he wore didn't hide the vivid blue of his eyes, which were currently popping out like a cartoon character's. "You look …" he repeated. I made it to the ground floor with a sigh of relief.

"Colleen, there are no words." Scott placed his hands on my shoulders and stood gazing at me, his eyes glittering behind the mask.

"Sure there are," Pat supplied as she came down the stairs. "Words like 'stunning,' 'ethereal,' 'gorgeous,' and 'ravishing,' to name a few." She stopped short when she noticed the necklace. "I didn't realize that you were going to wear that necklace," she remarked. She sounded upset. I immediately felt defensive.

"It's mine," I said stubbornly, like a petulant child. "I can wear it if I want to, and I couldn't think of a better occasion."

Pat held up her hands. "Of course, sure, I get it. Just, uh, be careful."

"Not to worry, she's in good hands," Scott said with a little bow, holding out his elbow. "Shall we, ladies?"

"We shall," I threw my shoulders back, held my chin up high, tucked my arm into Scott's, and we all trooped out the front doors to head for the town hall.

*   *   *

It always amazed me when the town hall was transformed into a glamorous and spooky wonderland for the ball. This was the room where they usually lined up the tables and discussed things like permits and zoning and other mundane items, but tonight the floor was obscured by roiling white fingers of mist pumping from the fog machines to curl around the ankles of the couples swirling and gyrating on the dance floor.

The air pulsed with music and the walls glowed from LED torches and the orange and yellow fairy lights strung overhead. Jack o' lanterns graced nearly every available surface, all entries in the annual pumpkin carving contest. The top three winners and the grand prize would be voted on by the ball attendees and announced at the end of the evening. Some were simple and classic with triangle noses and eyes, and others were elaborate carvings depicting entire scenes. My favorite so far was the carving of Nosferatu, the ancient vampire, stealing up a staircase, his bald head, hook nose, and elongated fangs prominent in his silhouette.

The long tables at the far end of the room were loaded down with trays of appetizers and baked goods. I recognized many items from MB Squared Bakery, including adorable petit fours. The tiny square cakes were decorated with everything autumn, including leaves and acorns as well as pumpkins, bats, and ghosts. I popped a white chocolate coated cake sporting a black spider web into my mouth. White chocolate and tart raspberries exploded in my mouth. I moaned happily.

"Would you care to dance?" Scott held his arm out. My mouth full, I could only nod. Scott led us onto the floor just as the Frank Sinatra tune "Witchcraft" began to play. Scott was a good dancer and a strong lead as we whirled around on the dance floor in an elevated box step.

I saw Pat dancing with Jeremiah Strong, the assistant manager of the Fresh Stop. Jeremiah was handsome and he was also about 25 years old. I grinned, thinking that Pat must be taking her duties seriously as a member of the Cougar Brigade. The song was over far too soon, and when I heard the next song, I thanked Scott for the dance and excused myself. I was not ready to get down to "Dragula" by Rob Zombie this early in the evening.

Scott moved to follow me as I exited the dance floor, but he was intercepted by Darlene from the El diner. She scooped him up and started gyrating around him like the moon spinning around the earth. I laughed and shook my head as I made my way to the back tables.

The green-hued punch was decorated with dry ice and large plastic spiders floated on the surface. I grabbed a clear plastic cup and scooped some out, game to try the concoction. I sipped gingerly at first. It was a creamy lemon-lime drink, and I took a larger gulp. I felt a tap on my shoulder and turned around.

"Mayor Reese, good evening! You look wonderful." I looked the mayor up and down. His midnight-blue tuxedo, accented with a blue velvet tie and cumberbun, was exquisite. It had to be designer, maybe even custom made. "Where's Rayna? I'll bet she looks stunning."

The mayor's mouth turned down at the corners, and I could see that his eyes were strained with worry behind his blue velvet mask. "Hello, Colleen, you look absolutely magnificent tonight. That necklace looks splendid on you."

He cleared his throat and leaned in closer. "I was coming over to ask if you've seen Rayna today. She hasn't shown up yet, and she never misses the ball. Her date hasn't heard from her all day, either."

I put a reassuring hand on his arm. "I'm sure she's just chasing a hot lead on a story. You know Rayna."

The mayor smiled weakly. "Yes, I know my Rayna. That girl is like a bloodhound once she senses a story. You're probably right." He briefly squeezed my hand and then stepped away to greet a woman in a deep purple satin gown overlaid with a black lacy fabric covered in a spider web pattern.

I moved through the crowd, sipping my punch and listening to the music. I saw that Scott was still trapped on the dance floor with several members of the Cougar Brigade. As I passed by the doorway that led to the hall where the restrooms were located, a hand shot out and grabbed my arm above the elbow. I was dragged into the hallway and nearly spilled the remainder of my punch.

"Ack!" I cried, yanking my arm away.

"I need to talk to you, it's important!" Jared's voice hissed in my ear.

"Jared Baumgarnter, let me go, right *now*," I insisted, still pulling away. Jared was not dressed for the ball. He was wearing his usual fare of worn jeans and plaid shirt, but he was rumpled, as if he had been wearing the same clothes for days.

His eyes were wild and he was breathing heavily. I stopped struggling and looked into his eyes.

"Jared, are you all right? You don't look very well," I told him.

"Listen, please, you've got to listen to me," he pleaded. His fingers dug painfully into my upper arm.

"Ow, Jared, you're hurting me," I whimpered. He immediately released his grip, but he stayed poised with his hands up and he continued to watch me warily, as if I were a frightened animal that might make a break for it at any second.

"Don't run," he said, as if reading my mind. "It's about Scott."

"No, I'm not doing this," I said firmly, turning to go. Jared grabbed my elbow, more gently this time.

"Please, listen, he isn't even Scott, his name is Gerald Lee Clemmonds. He has a criminal record for fraud and all kinds of nasty things, he—"

I wrenched my arm free from his grasp. My voice was ice cold and clipped. "Stop this right now, Jared. I won't hear of it. If the things you're saying were true, he would be in jail. You've got the wrong guy. Scott is a good person. He even gave up his own dog to make a family with children happy."

Jared's face fell and the light in his eyes dimmed. "Colleen, why won't you believe me? I've known you since the first grade, when Mrs. Valchuck put us in the same reading group together. You know me. I wouldn't lie to you," he pleaded. "What if the dog wasn't really his to begin with? He's using you, can't you see it?"

His eyes came to rest on the necklace. "You're wearing the ruby," he stated flatly.

"Why shouldn't I? Scott suggested …" I trailed off, recalling that it had been Scott who had first brought up the idea of me wearing the necklace to the ball. I shook my head, clearing the negative idea from my mind.

"You see?" Jared demanded, throwing both his hands up in frustration. "You're playing right into his hands!"

Fury filled me like liquid filling a jar, black and thick. "Of course, it couldn't just be me that he's interested in, because I'm too boring and ugly, is that right?"

I was so angry that I couldn't even see straight. I shoved Jared in the center of his chest, and he stumbled back a few steps.

"Don't follow me, Jared. I'm with Scott now, and you're not going to sabotage that just because you're pathologically jealous. I'm going back to the ball and I'm going to enjoy my evening with Scott."

As I turned, Jared reached for me again, but another partygoer passed between us, heading for the restrooms. I hurried back down the hall to the ballroom, my vision blurred by hot, angry tears. I blinked rapidly, trying to preserve Pat's excellent makeup.

In my hurry, I almost ran smack into Lacey. She was talking to Mikki in front of the food tables. Lacey wore a red gown with tiny black bats embroidered on the bodice and her mask was in the shape of a bat. Her red gold curls were piled high on top of her head like the Bride of Frankenstein. She grinned as I approached, then sobered when she saw my face.

"Girl, what's wrong? You look way too beautiful to be upset."

"Thanks," I replied, lifting my mask to dab at my eyes. "I just ran into Jared. He's got some sort of grudge against Scott for some reason," I explained.

Lacey smiled reassuringly. "Do your best to let it go. Tonight is your night." She turned to Mikki. "Get her a cookie, stat," she ordered.

Mikki, in a white wedding dress that she had torn and stained to look like a zombie bride, grabbed a cardamom-orange cookie and thrust it into my hand. "Your favorite." She looked at her boyfriend on the dance floor and said, "I'd better go and rescue Michael. If it wasn't for Scott, the poor guy would get no rest from that gang of senior man-eaters."

Before working her way onto the dance floor, she turned back to me. "You really do look absolutely stunning tonight, Colleen. That necklace is really something." Mikki waved and left me standing there with Lacey.

"Don't move," Lacey insisted. "Martin's been looking for you. I'm texting him to come find us by the punchbowl." She had to shout over the synthesizer riff from the song "Spooky" by the Atlanta Rhythm Section.

I ate my cookie, savoring the warmth of the cardamom contrasting with the bright orange flavor and letting the sugar course through my veins. A few minutes later, Martin emerged from the crowd.

"Let's go outside," he shouted. "I want to talk to you and Pat. Where is she?"

I glanced around and pointed. Pat was still on the dance floor, doing the Time Warp with Darlene and the rest of the poker club/Cougar Brigade.

"I guess I'll fill her in later," Martin remarked as he pulled Lacey and me along behind him, heading for the doors. We finally worked our way through the throngs of partiers and emerged into the clear, cool night air.

The stars were hard diamonds glittering in an expanse of black velvet sky. The skeletal arms of the trees waved in front of the glow from the street lights, obscuring pieces of the fat yellow moon suspended overhead, creating spooky shadows on the sidewalks below. Forks of lightning shot through the banks of silver clouds moving in from the northeast. It looked like a doozy of a storm was moving in.

"Whew, I really hate crowds," Martin said, wiping his brow.

Lacey leaned against him. "Try wearing four inch heels," she teased. Martin supported her as he escorted her to the nearest bench and eased her down onto it with a quick kiss. Their genuine respect and affection for one another warmed my heart even as I shivered from the chill of the October night in my off the shoulder gown. I hugged myself and rubbed my arms. The air was crisp and a breeze had picked up. The temperature had dropped significantly since we had arrived at the ball.

"What did you want to talk to me about?" I asked through chattering teeth. A cold front was definitely moving in with the impending storm.

"I looked into Ezra McIntyre's death, like Pat asked me to," Martin replied. "And it looks like she was right. There were several eyewitness accounts recorded—in very obscure places, mind you—that Ezra was found at the bottom of the stairs, not hanging from them as was reported by the papers at the time." He lifted an eyebrow. "The papers were quite sensationalistic back then."

"I know, there was a lot of creative journalism in the n-nineteenth century," I stuttered. "Was there an aut-topsy d-done?" I rocked from foot to foot, trying to keep warm.

"Such as it was back in the day," Martin replied. "The cause of death was a broken neck, which is probably how the hanging rumor got started. You're turning blue, let's go back inside."

"What about Ezra? Can we make s-s-some kind of announcement to clarify his d-death?" I asked.

"I suppose we can try to have something printed in the *Courier*," Martin said, hauling Lacey to her feet.

"Th-that would be g-g-great," I shivered.

"Interestingly, that was also Sarah's cause of death, a broken neck. Makes you wonder," Martin remarked as we reentered the building. I barely registered what he said, because I was basking in the blessed warmth. Thank goodness for central heating. I hadn't even brought a wrap or coat because it hadn't been so chilly earlier.

An arm snaked around my shoulders and I instinctively pulled away.

"Jared, if you think for one second—"

"Darling, it's me," Scott said, turning me around to face him. "I've been looking all over for you. You're practically turning purple, where have you been?" He peeled his jacket off and draped it over my shoulders. I burrowed into the warmth remaining from his body heat and breathed in his delightful scent of amber and musk and leather.

"I stepped outside to talk with Martin and Lacey," I replied.

"Oh, what about?" Scott asked casually. I hesitated, given the fact that he had blown up about paranormal ideas before.

"Just wedding stuff," I replied breezily. "Lacey wanted some opinions on decor, and since I just finished decorating the inn, she thought that I might have some insight and maybe some contacts that would be useful to her, even though of course decorating a wedding and an inn are very different." My mouth really was a runaway train when I was nervous. I gulped and made a herculean effort to stop talking.

"I hope you don't have your heart set on any more dancing," Scott told me. "I'm worn out from dancing with that group of ladies." He wiped his brow. "In fact, I was hoping that you might be ready to leave."

"Leave?" I cried. "We just got here! They haven't done the awards for the jack o' lanterns yet, or crowned the Harvest King and Queen."

Scott leaned forward and whispered in my ear. "I want to take you home. I have something very important to discuss with you about the future. Our future."

Goose pimples broke out over every inch of my skin. Scott wanted us to have a future! My heart sang and I forgot about being cold and my shoes pinching my feet. I was suspended in a pink and fluffy cloud of euphoria. My lips parted to tell Scott that of course I would leave with him, when I was suddenly pinned in place by a gigantic beam of blinding white light. The DJ's voice boomed over the loudspeaker.

"And there she is, our undisputed Harvest Queen, Colleen Perkins! Give it up for Colleen and the fabulous McKinney ruby!"

The crowd exploded into raucous applause, and I was suddenly lifted by my elbows as two burley men in red tuxedos guided me onto the stage. Michael Brandon was already there, the apparent Harvest King. He smiled sheepishly at me and shrugged, as if to say none of this was his idea. Mayor Reese stepped up to the microphone.

"I would like to thank everyone for coming to this year's Harvest Moon Masquerade. It's my pleasure to crown Michael Brandon and Colleen Perkins as this year's Harvest King and Queen!"

He turned to Mindy Cranston, who was wearing a cloud-gray strapless gown with a tight bodice that flared out into layers of darker gray tulle. Mindy held a red velvet pillow on which rested two plastic gold crowns. The mayor picked up the larger crown and set it on Michael's head, where it promptly slid over his eyes.

Michael discreetly pushed the plastic brim back and blinked his ice-blue eyes in the glare of the spotlight. At least my crown fit me somewhat better; maybe my braids were holding it up.

Michael and I smiled and stood for a picture with the mayor and several of the two of us. I couldn't see past the black wall created by the stage lights, but I could hear the cheers and shouts from the crowd and feel the surge of their energy coming at me. The moment was surreal, but I couldn't help but wish that Scott had been up here with me.

As we descended the stage, a circle of bodies surrounded me and pats on the back and shoulder, hugs, and hand squeezes and murmurs of congratulations came at me fast and furious. I felt the room closing in on me, and my breathing was shallow and rapid and the room was suddenly blazing hot. I was panicking. A pair of strong, slim hands shot out and grasped my shoulders. I was pulled against a very fine and firm chest and recognized the amber musk of Scott's scent. My hands turned into claws and clung to his lapels.

"Get me out of here," I gasped. Without a word, Scott actually scooped me up into his arms and the press of bodies parted like the Red Sea as Scott carried me across the ballroom, like Richard Gere and Debra Winger in *An Officer and a Gentleman*. I would have swooned if I wasn't already off my feet.

The crown slipped off my head and hit the ground with a clatter as it rolled away. Scott didn't break stride, and as we approached the doors, they were opened by someone and the night air hit my face like an icy slap after the stuffiness of the ballroom. I shivered in Scott's arms and he pulled me closer against his chest. I pressed my ear to him, and I could faintly hear the beating of his heart, in spite of the roar of the wind. The storm was moving closer.

"Can you stand for a moment while I get the car door open?" Scott asked, leaning close to my ear, causing me to shudder.

Unable to speak, I bobbed my head up and down.

Scott set me gently on my feet and I released my grasp on the lapels of his jacket. He got the passenger door open and eased me onto the seat.

As we drove the deserted streets to the inn, I observed the wind blowing the leaves about and flapping the decorations and signs violently. Periodically, flashes of lightning would illuminate the road, followed by the rumbling boom of thunder. I was suddenly very glad that we had left the ball when we did so that we could beat the storm home.

Home. I had been searching for my true home ever since my father had passed away. I had thought of home as a place, but I now understood that it was really a feeling and a person or relationship that defined home.

I glanced over at Scott, who was absorbed in navigating the wind-blown streets. His square jaw and sloping nose and waving hair tousled by the blowing gale already felt dear to me.

My home.

I leaned back against the seat, sighing with contentment and feeling more hopeful about the future than I had in a long time.

Chapter 14

As we pulled up in front of the inn, the storm broke. Fat drops of rain splattered on the hood and windshield, followed by sheets of water. The rattle of hail on the roof startled me. Scott cursed under his breath as the hard white balls of ice hit and bounced off of the hood. He took off his suit jacket and handed it to me.

"Here, put this over your head when you get out. I'll come around and open your door and we'll make a dash for the house."

I took the jacket and when Scott opened my door, it was wrenched out of his hands by the force of the blowing gale. The door creaked loudly as it was slammed all the way open, the hinges crying out in protest. Scott grabbed my arm and we ran in a stumbling tangle up the front path and up the porch stairs.

The inn had never seemed so warm and welcoming and peaceful as we burst through the doors, dripping and laughing.

"Whew, that's some storm brewing," I said, shaking off droplets and bits of ice from my skirts. "I should run up and change."

Scott stopped me with a hand on my arm. "Please don't, not yet. I'd like to have a nightcap with you, by the fire, and enjoy you just like this." His eyes traveled up and down, from my head to my toes and back again, coming to rest on my face. "Please," he added. "Just for a while, let me admire you like this."

My throat dried up and I could barely croak out, "Okay."

"Wonderful! I've laid a fire in the east parlor, if you would be so good as to light it, I'll fix us a night cap."

Scott headed for the kitchen while I carefully hung his jacket on the coat hook in the front hall. Bennie, Mac, and Henley were all huddled in the east parlor. I was sure that the cats, Lemon and Lime, were also hiding out from the storm together somewhere.

I jumped and the dogs all whimpered as the house shook with the sharp crack and vibration of thunder directly following a burst of blue lightning. Bennie tried to crawl his large body underneath the couch as the lights all went black. *Power's out.*

I felt along the mantle until my fingers found the tube of long fireplace matches. I fumbled the tube open and struck the match. I touched the flame to the kindling in the fireplace as the acrid smell of sulfur permeated the air around me.

Scott entered the parlor carrying a tall mug in each hand.

"Luckily, I got the water heated just before the power went out, although I almost tripped and spilled everything stumbling through the house." he said, holding one of the mugs out to me. It was frothy and dusted with dark powder, whatever it was.

"Cappuccino?" I asked, accepting the mug.

"Mexican hot chocolate, with whipped cream and a sprinkling of cinnamon," Scott replied. "My own secret recipe."

"Mmm, sounds delicious." I settled onto the couch with my mug, kicking off my heels and settling back with my mug. I sipped gingerly. The liquid was chocolaty and rich and slightly spicy, with a slightly bitter aftertaste. Scott was anxiously watching me, and I guessed that he was eager for my reaction to his drink recipe. I took another swallow. "It's good," I told him. He beamed at me.

"It's just what you need on a dark and stormy night. Drink up." He held his own mug up. "Here's to the Harvest Queen!"

I laughed and clicked my mug gently against his and we both took sips.

"I'm still in shock," I admitted. "Never in my wildest dreams did I think I would be named Harvest Queen. I mean, Michael Brandon makes sense. He's established a great business in town, he's been on TV, he's dating a hometown girl, not to mention that he's such a doll. But me, I'm nobody, just a plain old innkeeper."

Scott was staring at me, the firelight casting deep and disconcerting shadows on his face, elongating and sharpening his features, making him appear sinister. He spoke, and his teeth gleamed in the orange glow. His eyes were pools of shadow and unreadable.

I put the mug down on the coffee table. I had fibbed a bit when I had told Scott that it tasted good. I was put off by the strange bitter aftertaste.

Scott quickly held his mug up again. "Would it be too soon to propose a toast to us?"

"I think I would like that very much," I replied, lifting my mug and tapping it against his.

"To us," he repeated as he looked deeply into my eyes. He seemed to be searching for something. We lifted the cups to our lips.

I tipped mine and touched my lips to the liquid, but only pretended to take a drink. It really did taste off somehow. Maybe the milk had gone sour. Scott didn't seem to mind the taste of his hot chocolate, because he drank deeply.

I felt suddenly shy, conscious of the gothic atmosphere of the pounding storm outside and the dark and empty mansion where I was alone with Scott. I turned toward the fireplace and concentrated on staring at the dancing flames. My eyelids were becoming too heavy for me to hold open. I blinked and my eyelids felt like rough sandpaper against my eyeballs.

"I'm so sleepy all of a sudden," I murmured, my words slurring slightly. "I must have tired myself out with all the excitement tonight." I tried to rise from the couch, but my limbs felt like weighted blankets holding me in place. I was numb and my tongue was swelling with a metallic taste.

"Scott?" My eyes rolled sideways, seeking his face. He stared at me, his blue eyes hard and glinting in the firelight. I became frightened that he wasn't trying to help me and didn't seem concerned.

"Scott, what's happening to me?" I could barely raise my voice above a whisper. My lips burned. I was confused and terrified that my limbs were somehow incapable of obeying the signal from my brain to move.

My head lolled against the back of the couch as Scott stood over me and leaned in close. He snapped his fingers inches from my face, but all I could do was lift my chin slightly. He stood upright with a satisfied air, smiling broadly.

"Finally," he cried. "I don't think that I could have put up with your simpering and whining and constant babbling for much longer."

He began to pace up and down in front of the fire. His voice didn't sound the same. It had a hard edge now, with a higher pitch. He shook a finger at me. "You don't know how many times you almost made me blow my cover, with your annoying habits and silly meandering speeches."

I knew that if my body were capable of feeling anything right now, my heart would be breaking. As it was, I could only roll my eyes toward Scott as tears filled my vision. I struggled to speak because my tongue was like felted wool stuffed into my mouth.

I managed to choke out a single word. "Why?"

Scott abruptly stopped pacing and rushed toward me and bent forward, his face next to mine. I felt a deep chill of fear despite the numbness in my body when Scott began to laugh maniacally as his hot cinnamon-scented breath washed over me.

"You really are as stupid as you are repulsive and annoying, aren't you?" He giggled, and it was an ugly, high-pitched sound. "I saw an article in that insipid rag you call a newspaper and fitted myself up as a travel writer and the man of your dreams. Did you really think that I was attracted to *you*? There are plenty of mirrors around here. Try looking in one."

He waved his hands in the air. "Better yet, record yourself talking. You may be boring and unattractive, but you do have one good quality."

He leaned over and grasped the ruby nestled at my throat. I moaned as the clasp pinched the nape of my neck when Scott yanked the ruby and ripped the necklace off of me, taking strands of my hair with it. Scott held the necklace up, the giant faceted ruby dangling before the fire, gleaming with a light of its own. He whistled through his teeth and grinned like a shark.

"I'll never have to pull off another score again if I play this one right," he muttered as he shoved the necklace into his pocket. From the depths of another pocket, his phone began to ring. He dug the phone out and answered it with a whoop.

"I got it, baby! We're set for life!"

I could faintly hear the sound of a female voice screaming for joy. Scott's face was distorted with an ugly, sly smile. He listened for a moment as the female voice spoke.

"Baby," he replied, "I'm taking you to the Maldives and we're gonna live on a yacht and drink rum punch and lie in the sun all day." He glanced briefly at me as the voice droned again, and then he said, "No problem, she's almost totally out. Meet me in ten minutes at the corner of Oak and Main. I'll take care of her, just like I took care of that other nosey woman." He hung up with those chilling words.

I could feel the wetness on my cheeks from crying and I was aware that my dogs were still huddled in the corner, unconcerned about me since I just appeared to be sleepy. I wanted to thrash, to scream, to fight, to do anything, but I was helpless as my consciousness faded to a pinpoint of light. I struggled to stay alert, but the pinpoint grew smaller until it disappeared, swallowed by the blackness.

*   *   *

"Daddy, no!" I shrieked. "I love him!"

The man before me was looming over me on the top stair, waving a small red leather bound book.

"Love," he spat. "Who cares about love? The Hunnicut fortune was our only hope, and you've gone and thrown everything away for love." He hurled the journal at me, and I held my hands up feebly to deflect the blow. I knew that he must have found the letter hidden under the binding, the letter from my true love.

"I don't care, I'll go away—with Franklin—and you'll never have to see me again," I pleaded. The man who was my father laughed, his gravelly voice rattling in his throat.

"You're not going anywhere with that low-class mutt, because he's dead. I made sure of it, and the only place you'll find him is buried under the oak tree."

My heart didn't break, it simply dissolved. I lost all sensation, all concern, and my will to live drained from my body like sap from a tree.

"No," I said flatly. "It can't be true."

"Do you think I wanted to do it? It was the only way I could think of to get the marriage done. No daughter of mine is marrying a working class caretaker. You won't run away from this. You're marrying Hunnicut next week, and that is my final word as the master of this house!"

He reached out and grabbed for my shoulders, to shake me. I stumbled back from him, dreading his touch. My foot came down on air instead of the wooden stair. I felt myself going over, losing my balance. My father's hands reached out and I caught his wrists for a brief moment. He began pulling me toward him. I thought of my lost beloved, and as I looked into the cold and calculating eyes of the man who had ruled my entire life, the man who would sell me into a life of loveless misery for cold, hard cash, I smiled. His eyes widened.

"Sarah, you would not dare," he growled.

I released my grip and relaxed into the arms of gravity, falling backward, as my father screamed my name.

*   *   *

As I dreamed of hitting the floor at the bottom of the stairs head-first, my body jolted and my eyelids fluttered open. I was lying on the floor in a darkened room. The ground felt like packed dirt. It was cold to the touch and smelled of earth.

My head pounded and felt as if it were stuffed with cotton, and my mouth was dry as sand. The storm continued to rage outside, howling around the walls and screaming into the nooks and crannies. I struggled to sit up, feeling around in the darkness.

I reasoned that if the storm was still going, not much time could have passed since Scott had drugged my hot chocolate. I shook off the wild dream—or was it a vision?—and tried to gather my wits.

I crawled around in my gown, inwardly groaning that I was ruining it, but that was really the least of my concerns right now. My hands finally landed on something soft and squishy, that was also smooth and yet lumpy. A strap extended from it. A purse! It had to be a purse. I fumbled for the zipper and got the bag open. I felt around the interior for anything that I could use to help with my situation.

My fingers closed on something metallic, cylindrical, and long, with a larger point at one end. I prayed it was a flashlight. I ran my fingers along, and found a button. I pushed it and the end flared with light. My eyes were used to the blackness and I grimaced, squinting. I shone the light around the walls. They were made of blocks of soot-stained stones held together with crumbling mortar. There was a square opening high up on the long end of the wall and another larger opening in the opposite long wall.

I figured that I must be in an old coal cellar. When the houses were heated by coal, the delivery man would bring the coal and dump it through the smaller chute from outside, and then the family could access the coal through the larger chute as they needed. There must be some sort of door, for cleaning out the cellar or something, I reasoned to myself as I began feeling along the walls.

A groan from the corner startled me so much that I nearly dropped the flashlight. If I wasn't so groggy from whatever drug Scott had given me, I would have wondered where the purse had come from. I swung the flashlight beam toward the sound. I saw a tangle of jet black hair.

To my astonishment, Rayna Reese lay in a crumpled heap in the corner, moaning. I rushed over to her.

"Rayna, how hurt are you?" I ran my hands anxiously over her form, feeling for anything broken or bloody. She brushed my hands away and struggled to sit up.

"Colleen?" she asked, blinking in the beam of the flashlight. "What happened? How did we get here?" She had what looked like the beginning of a large bruise just above her right temple.

"I assume that Scott put me in here, after he drugged my hot chocolate," I replied. "I don't know about you."

Rayna pushed herself to a sitting position and leaned against the wall. "I was investigating him. He had to be lying. He was just too cute to be into you, I'm sorry."

She did not sound very sorry to me.

"I tried to tell you, that day at the dry cleaners. I was going to spill everything, but then Scott—I mean, Gerald—caught me going through the glove compartment in his rental car." She rubbed her head and winced. "The next thing I remember is waking up in here with you." She glanced around. "Where are we?"

"I think we're in the old coal cellar of the inn. If there was a larger door, it must have been sealed off, I wasn't even aware it was here," I said.

The room shook as a thunderclap boomed overhead. Rayna screamed and I jumped.

"Calm down, it's just thunder," I told her. "We've got to find a way to get out of here. If I didn't know the coal cellar was here, nobody else will, and even if they come looking, they may not find us right away."

Rayna settled back against the wall. "No thanks, I'll wait. We can just scream our heads off when someone arrives."

"I don't suppose you've got a phone in your purse?" I asked.

"That jerk smashed it when he found me," she growled. "He owes me a grand!"

I rolled my eyes, which made me feel queasy with the after effects of whatever drug I had been given. "That's not the top of our priority list," I scolded. "At least you had a flashlight."

"Whatever. I have a Luna bar in my bag. Want half?"

"No, I want you to help me find a way out of here," I said through my teeth.

"Someone will come," Rayna said with flat certainty.

I wish I had her faith. I was already feeling claustrophobic in the small windowless room. I reasoned that if I started looking for an exit, maybe Rayna would join in. I crept along the baseboard area, shining the light as I went, probing for anything out of the ordinary.

I saw the bulk of an object in the coal bin that accessed the house. I lifted the flashlight over my head and peered in then leaped back with a strangled cry as I spotted blue jeans and red sneakers draped over white bone.

Rayna looked up from her protein bar. "What is it?" she asked.

"It can't be, but it looks like the remains of a person. A person who was very small," I replied with a shudder.

I suddenly flashed on the missing boy from 1985. It was entirely possible that his family was also not aware of the existence of the coal cellar, and the boy had stumbled across it and fallen or climbed in and been trapped somehow. The thought crept in that if he had cried out for help, no one had been able to hear him, which would put a serious dent in Rayna's plan to be rescued.

"A body? But, who?" Rayna demanded.

"I think it might be the boy who disappeared on the property in the 80s," I said grimly. "It's skeletonized now, but I'm sure there are tests that can be done to—" I broke off and sniffed the dank air. "Do you smell smoke?"

Rayna inhaled sharply through her nostrils. I noticed that she had soot and dirt smeared across her face, her makeup was smeared and her hair was sticking out like a rat's nest. She still looked roughly beautiful somehow.

"I do," she replied, and her violet eyes widened with animal fear. "Do you think Gerald set the house on fire?"

"Who the heck is Gerald?" I was exasperated that Rayna could never focus on anything.

"That's Scott's real name, Gerald Lee Clemmonds," Rayna explained. I recalled Jared trying to warn me about

Scott, and he had mentioned that name, too. The thought of Jared, with his solid presence and familiar face, made me want to start crying again. Why couldn't I have just believed him when he tried to tell me the truth? Why had my ego refused to let me see what was right in front of my face?

"I don't know if it was Scott—uh, Gerald—or that last lightning strike, but we need to get out of here, now. Can you stand on your own?" I strode over to Rayna and stood over her, ready to help her up.

"Ugh, not to mention, we're stuck in here with a dead person," Rayna shivered violently. To her credit, with a lot of effort involving getting on her hands and knees and doing a shimmy up the wall with her hands, she did get to her feet eventually.

"I broke two nails," she cried in dismay.

"If we get out of here, I'm going to kill you, Rayna," I stated flatly. "You can get all the manicures you want later, just focus on escaping right now."

The smell of smoke grew stronger as we prodded along the walls of the cellar room. I thought of my animals upstairs, and fought back my panic for their safety. I needed to keep my wits about me at the moment. It was the best chance of saving them.

Finally, I deduced that it was likely that Rayna and I had been shoved through the larger chute, over where the boy's remains lay. My stomach roiled at the thought. It took everything I had, but I gritted my teeth and poked around to see if the way in could also be the way out. The chute appeared to work only 'in' and the push door only swung inwards, into the cellar. When pushing failed, I tried to dig my fingertips under the edge and pull it back toward me, but I couldn't get a decent grip.

I looked at the other chute, on the opposite wall. It was smaller, and it may only open inwards as well, but it was our last chance.

"Rayna, I'm going to boost you up there," I pointed with the beam of the flashlight. "Then I want you to see if you can push the door outwards, and I'll shove you through."

"Why can't you do it?" Rayna demanded, hands on hips.

"Because," I said slowly, "I am too large to fit through that opening."

"Right," Rayna said, and she had the grace to look somewhat embarrassed in the periphery of the flashlight.

I made a basket with my hands and Rayna stepped up. As soon as she had a grasp on the sill of the door, I shifted and hugged her knees, using my shoulder to boost her up.

"It's a little metal door," she reported. "It opens outward!"

I heard a creak as she pushed the door open.

"Are you in?" I asked. "Should I start pushing?" I grunted with the effort of holding her up there. I was seconds from dropping her, so I just started shoving.

"Hey, ow, there's a huge prickly bush up here," Rayna cried in protest, but I didn't care. This was our only hope. I could feel Rayna's weight sliding back toward me as I lost my grip. Desperate, I gave one final mighty push. I collapsed, expecting Rayna to tumble down on top of me. When she didn't, I picked up the flashlight and saw her legs dangling from high on the wall.

"I'm stuck," her muffled voice yelled. "Push me again!"

I stood and tried to reach her feet, but they were too high up. I jumped, but I couldn't close the gap.

"I can't reach you," I called out, hoping she could hear me, since her top half was outside. *Her top half was outside!* "Rayna, scream your head off! Maybe someone will hear you!" I called out, making a megaphone with my hands. I started coughing as the smoke thickened. My eyes streamed and burned.

"Help! We're trapped in the basement of the inn! HELP!!" Rayna screamed.

I had lost all concept of time, and I had no idea how long Rayna screamed as she hung halfway through the coal chute, but just as her voice was going hoarse, I heard the blessed sound of sirens approaching from a distance. If Scott/Gerald had set fire to the house to cover his tracks, it had backfired, no pun intended. Someone must have seen the smoke and called the fire department.

Suddenly, Rayna's feet were yanked upwards and her lower half disappeared. A moment later, Jared's face peered through the small opening.

"Colleen?" he called.

I could have wept with relief at the sight of his round face. "Jared, I'm here!" I yelled.

"Colleen, the roof is on fire! I need to get you out." His face disappeared, and an arm replaced it, waving. "Take my hand, I'll pull you up."

"I can't fit," I yelled. "Rayna barely fit through."

The arm disappeared. The face returned. "I'm coming in. Gerald barricaded the doors, so I might have to break a window," Jared warned.

"Do what you have to, just get the animals out," I told him. "I'm in the old coal cellar, but I have no idea how to find it from upstairs, but there must be stairs or something, because Scott found it."

"Right," he said, and vanished again.

I paced the packed dirt floor anxiously as I wrung my hands. It was torture to be able to do nothing but wait. I could hear banging on the floor above me as the sirens drew nearer.

Just as I was about to burst with anxiety, there was a crash and a sliver of light as the larger coal door was pushed inward.

"Colleen, are you there?" Jared called. "Oh my God, I think there's a body in here," he muttered in amazement.

"Yes, there is, and yes, I'm here! Now get me out of here! We'll figure out the body later."

I can't pull you through, this is one way only," he replied. "I'm going to have to break the wall down."

"What? How?" I cried.

"I grabbed some tools from my truck," Jared yelled through the wall.

I heard the clang of metal against stone. I stepped back against the opposite wall and watched as the stones began to vibrate with the force of the blows. The crumbling old mortar was giving way and disintegrating. The clanging stopped for a second, and then I heard the solid thud of what sounded like a sledgehammer. I crouched down and covered my face with my arms as the stones gave way and collapsed into a heap, exposing a huge hole in the wall. I ran into Jared's arms without hesitation. He scooped me up, threw me over his shoulder in a fireman's carry and dashed up the narrow staircase. He didn't put me down until we were outside across the street. The rain had stopped and the wind had died down to a stiff breeze. My stockings were torn and my left big toe stuck out. I knew that the rest of me must have been a sight to behold.

Rayna stood there placidly holding the leashes of my dogs, while the cats yowled from inside the cab of Jared's pickup. I was overjoyed to see that they were all okay, and I dropped to my knees, hugging my dogs as they whined and licked my face. Thank goodness the inn was empty of guests, since everyone had gone to the ball.

My neighbor, Mrs. Jenkins, wrapped a blanket around my shoulders as I stood up.

"Don't you worry, they caught it in time. You'll have some repairs ahead, but you won't lose the house," she assured me. "Would you like some hot chocolate?"

"No, thank you," I said with a shiver. I would probably never be able to enjoy hot chocolate again.

A black pickup roared up and Lacey and Mikki leaped out, followed by Michael and Martin. Lacey rushed to me, high heels be damned, and threw her arms around me.

"Colleen, we heard the call go out for the fire department! I was so scared for you. Are you alright?"

I couldn't respond because she had my face pressed into her shoulder, and then Mikki arrived to throw her arms around the both of us. She was crying and rocking us from side to side. I finally managed to extract myself from the Lacey-Mikki sandwich and take a breath of the cool, damp night air tinged with smoke.

"Guys, I'm okay, and the inn should be okay, too."

Darlene's pink Cadillac screeched up behind the pickup, and Pat popped out before the car stopped rolling. She came directly to me and grabbed me by the shoulders.

"Don't ever scare me like this again," she said, shaking me, then yanking me to her and hugging me fiercely. I had never been squeezed so much in my life.

"What happened? Where's Scott?" Mikki asked, wiping her eyes with the sleeve of her gown.

I sighed. "Long story short, I fell for a long con, apparently. Scott was pretending to be Scott, he was just after the necklace all along." My fingers trailed up to my naked throat. I wasn't even that upset about the monetary value. I was far more devastated about the history and the connection to my ancestors that was lost. "At least he didn't set the fire, that was courtesy of the lightning from the storm."

"Oh, honey, I'm so sorry," Lacey said, drawing me in for another long hug. Mikki hiccuped and Michael pulled her closer.

Pat's lips compressed in a grim line. "I had a bad feeling about that character," she stated. "He tried to talk me into writing him a check for ten thousand bucks, he said it was an 'investment opportunity.'" She harrumphed. "As if I would ever give the likes of him a single dime."

"We're just glad you're not hurt," Michael told me. Martin agreed.

"Martin, I have to tell you that I had the oddest dream while I was unconscious," I said. I told them the story of what I had seen in my dream, and Martin stroked his beard thoughtfully.

"The events are certainly plausible, though we may never be able to prove what really happened. I can, however, make some contacts and set up a dig under the oak tree." His eyes gazed off into the distance. "There was a payroll entry from the estate ledger for a caretaker named F. James, you know."

"I didn't know that. You'd think it has to be the same man," I replied.

"Depends on the time period, and whether there are records of him existing elsewhere after the events surrounding Sarah's demise and her family leaving the area," Martin cautioned.

Jared appeared, looking disheveled and slightly singed. He had been talking with the firefighters, and he reiterated what Mrs. Jenkins had said. The fire had started when lightning struck the belvedere. The rain had helped keep the flames at bay somewhat, and the blaze was soon extinguished by the firefighters and the damage was contained to the western roof.

"Jared," I clutched his arm, "Scott's getting away, he stole the necklace, and some lady is picking him up at Oak and Main, and he's going to get away."

Jared smiled placidly. "Nope, I called Deputy Willis as soon as I couldn't find you at the ball. He came straight this way, and encountered Scott or Gerald speeding down Oak and intercepted him. He's in the county lockup as we speak."

"What about the necklace?"

"Safely in the evidence lockup," Jared assured me.

I threw my arms around him and kissed him soundly on the cheek. "Thank you for saving us," I told him.

"You're a hero, man." Michael clapped Jared on the back.

Jared blushed so deeply we could see it even in the dim light of the streetlamp.

"I just beat the fire department here, they would have saved the day a few minutes later," he said modestly.

"But they didn't, you did." How could I have ever thought of Jared as plain and homely, as nothing more than a friend? He had always been there for me, he had always had my back. There were few people in my life that I could say the same about.

"You've always been one of my best friends," I said, letting the blanket slide off my shoulders and stepping in front of him as I placed my hands on his shoulders. "I'm so sorry that I didn't believe you when you tried to warn me about Scott. Or Gerald. Or whoever he is."

I slid my hands down to Jared's chest. I could feel his heart pounding under my palms. "Thank you for caring about me enough to jeopardize our friendship by telling me the truth, even when I refused to hear it." I reached up and placed my hands gently on either side of his face, his beard prickly against my hands.

"You ran into a burning building for me, Jared." My voice was thick with emotion as I looked into Jared's warm brown eyes. "Thank you for being such a good friend and a good man—one of the best I've ever known."

I stood on tiptoe and pressed my lips to his. His body stiffened in surprise, but it only took a few seconds before he wrapped his arms around me, pulled me close, and participated in the kiss with enthusiasm. The crowd of friends around us cheered and whistled. When we finally broke apart, Rayna was staring at us.

"So does this mean that I missed the ball?" she asked.

Epilogue

The soft, lavender-scented spring breeze lifted my hair off my shoulders. It was longer now, without extensions. Jared took my hand in his as we strolled toward the eastern section of the Pinewood Cemetery. In my other hand, I held a large basket of flowers.

"Do you think we brought enough?" I asked anxiously.

Jared squeezed my hand. "I'm sure we did, honey. And if not, I can run over to the florist for more." He pointed with his free hand. "There they are."

Martin and Lacey stood with Mikki and Michael and Pat, along with a man in a black suit. They were all gathered around an open grave. The black lacquered casket rested on a platform nearby. A spray of white roses adorned its gleaming top.

"Welcome, I'm Reverend Jim Maxwell." The man in the black suit stepped forward and shook our hands. "Now that we're all here, let's get started."

The reverend said a few words and quoted some Bible verses. We all bowed our heads during the prayer.

"And now we commit Franklin Elmer James to the earth," he finished. The casket was lowered into the ground and we all took turns placing a primrose from my basket into the grave. We made sure to place some on Sarah's grave right next door, too.

"Rest well together," Lacey said solemnly.

"I'm glad we found him, and we could reunite them, even in death," I murmured, running my hands over the top of Sarah Ellis's headstone.

"I'm glad that I got to publish my book and shed new light on their stories," Martin chimed in.

He had written a book called *The Lives and Deaths of the Harvest Moon Inn* and it had proved to be a popular story with the inn's guests. Martin's book detailed the suspected truths about how Ezra McIntyre had died by accident and had not hanged himself and how Sarah Ellis's greedy father was suspected of attempting to right his failing fortune by selling his daughter's youth and beauty to the highest bidder and destroying anyone in his way. It wasn't proof, but I was convinced in my own heart that my vision had been true. Sarah may not have hanged herself, but she had given up her life when she had realized that her true love was gone.

Martin's team had found her lover, Franklin James, buried under the oak tree behind the inn, under the primroses, just where Ellis had said he would be in my dream. We had decided that burying him next to Sarah was the right thing to do.

As far as the body in the coal chute, it was determined through DNA testing that it was indeed the missing boy from 1985, Timothy Beale. Timothy had his own chapter in Martin's book. Martin speculated the same thing that I did—that poor Timothy had somehow stumbled across the coal chute and had been trapped. His parents, Connie and Steven Beale, had been contacted and notified. When they had come to Pinewood Corners to arrange for the remains of their son to be transported to Ohio for burial, they had asked to meet with me.

We met at the Java Hut for coffee. They thanked me for bringing them closure in the disappearance of their son so many years ago, and we all shed a few tears for Timothy.

Now, Jared squeezed my shoulders. "Are you doing okay? Do you want to go spend some time at your dad's grave?"

"I'd like that," I said, leaning against his chest. "Then we can meet everybody back at the inn for dinner."

"Roger that," Pat said. "I told Mrs. Blake to have a meal ready at seven."

"Have you had any more paranormal issues at the inn?" Mikki asked.

Jared responded, "Nope, not any longer. Seems that uncovering the remains and the truth have quieted everything down."

"They just wanted their stories told," Pat insisted. "The spirits stuck around, hoping for someone to get the word out."

"I told you, remember?" Jared said.

"Told me what?" I asked, puzzled.

"That the house had a lingering darkness, and it needed hope to bring new light. You were the catalyst that brought hope to the house, and shed light on the darkness. Now the inn is filled with light and love."

"Ah, that's right."

It was ironic, I thought, that the evil actions of the con man and career criminal, Gerald Lee Clemmonds, AKA Scott Carpenter, were instrumental in uncovering the house's hidden remains and deepest secrets. I reflected that even though it was an awful experience to go through, I was thankful. What Scott had done had led to finding Timothy and Franklin, and this wealthy woman and her faithful handyman finally getting their happy ending.

I looked at Jared, with the sunlight in his hair, smiling at me with love in his eyes, and my heart swelled with gratitude.

"And, Jared, I believe that I said to you, 'Why Jared, that's beautiful, did I not?'"

"You did. And do you know what's even more beautiful?"

I leaned closer and before our lips met gently, I heard him whisper, "This moment with you." In an instant, the breeze picked up and primroses fluttered in the air all around us.

The End

About the Author

Carol Babineaux, who has always loved stories about love, has also been a lifelong fan of all things ghostly. Since Halloween is her favorite holiday, she felt inspired to intertwine this spooky season with the third installment of her Pinewood Corners Sweet Romance series.

Professionally, Carol has enjoyed a long career in administration and has a diploma in Integrated Healing and Hypnotherapy from the Southwest Institute of Healing Arts.

When she isn't writing or working, you can find her practicing yoga, reading, cooking, watching movies, or spending time with her family and friends. Carol currently resides in Arizona with her husband and their gaggle of cats.

carolbabineaux.com

The Pinewood Corners Sweet Romance Series

The Christmas Cookie Conundrum (Nov. 2023)
The St. Valentine's Situation (Feb. 2024)
The Harvest Moon's Hope (Oct. 2024)

Follow Carol on Amazon

Scan the QR code below or visit:
bit.ly/carolbabineaux

Do You Love Pinewood Corners Sweet Romance?

Let's Keep in Touch!

Be the first to get exclusive author updates, exciting book news, and other delightful surprises by visiting:

carolbabineaux.com/home

* 9 7 9 8 9 9 1 5 2 5 7 1 8 *